Miss Marcy Pruitt's Private To Do List:

1) Get away from demanding fans.

2) Take refuge in Wolf River, Texas: three weeks away from the crazy world to enjoy best friend's wedding.

3) Indulge in light flirtation with sexy-as-sin brother of the groom.

4) Change look so as not to be recognized by demanding manager.

5) Fall into bed with Evan Carter. (Note: Do _not_ fall in love with him!)

6) Rethink this affair before someone gets hurt.

Dear Reader,

Yes, we have what you're looking for at Silhouette Desire. This month, we bring you some of the most anticipated stories…and some of the most exciting new tales we have ever offered.

Yes, *New York Times* bestselling author Lisa Jackson is back with Randi McCafferty's story. You've been waiting to discover who fathered Randi's baby and who was out to kill her, and the incomparable Lisa Jackson answers all your questions and more in *Best-Kept Lies*. Yes, we have the next installment of DYNASTIES: THE DANFORTHS with Cathleen Galitz's *Cowboy Crescendo*. And you can be sure that wild Wyoming rancher Toby Danforth is just as hot as can be. Yes, there is finally another SECRETS! book from Barbara McCauley. She's back with *Miss Pruitt's Private Life*, a scandalous tale of passionate encounters and returning characters you've come to know and love.

Yes, Sara Orwig continues her compelling series STALLION PASS: TEXAS KNIGHTS with an outstanding tale of stranded strangers turned secret lovers, in *Standing Outside the Fire*. Yes, the fabulous Kathie DeNosky is back this month with a scintillating story about a woman desperate to have a *Baby at* His *Convenience*. And yes, Bronwyn Jameson is taking us down under as two passionate individuals square off in a battle that soon sweeps them *Beyond Control*.

Here's hoping you'll be saying "Yes, yes, yes" to Silhouette Desire all month…all summer…all year long!

Melissa Jeglinski

Melissa Jeglinski
Senior Editor
Silhouette Desire

Please address questions and book requests to:
Silhouette Reader Service
U.S.: 3010 Walden Ave., P.O. Box 1325, Buffalo, NY 14269
Canadian: P.O. Box 609, Fort Erie, Ont. L2A 5X3

BARBARA McCAULEY

Miss Pruitt's Private Life

Silhouette® Desire

Published by Silhouette Books

America's Publisher of Contemporary Romance

SILHOUETTE BOOKS

ISBN 0-373-76593-2

MISS PRUITT'S PRIVATE LIFE

Visit Silhouette Books at www.eHarlequin.com

Printed in U.S.A.

Books by Barbara McCauley

BARBARA McCAULEY,

who has written more than twenty novels for Silhouette Books, lives in Southern California with her own handsome hero husband, Frank, who makes it easy to believe in and write about the magic of romance. Barbara's stories have won and been nominated for numerous awards, including the prestigious RITA® Award from the Romance Writers of America, Best Desire of the Year from *Romantic Times* and Best Short Contemporary from the National Reader's Choice Awards.

One

Dear Marcy,
I am taking a train across the country from the
West Coast. I need to travel light, with a wardrobe
that will include casual to dressy. Do you have any
tips on how best to pack for a long trip, yet travel
light?
Angie in Anaheim

Marcy stared out the window of her private sleeper
car, watched the Texas landscape rumble by in a blur
of thick mesquite. July heat shimmered off the sparse
landscape, while cattle, mindless of the passing train,
grazed languidly under the midday sun. In the distance,
a tall metal windmill twirled like a child's toy in the hot,
summer breeze.

It was like looking at a picture postcard, Marcy
thought, resting her head back against the leather-up-
holstered seat. A deep blue sky. White, puffy clouds on

the distant horizon. The gentle rocking of the railroad car—

The shrill ring of her cell phone.

Fifteen hundred miles between herself and Los Angeles and still it wasn't enough.

Marcy glanced at her wristwatch. Eight-thirty L.A. time. She'd been waiting for the call, knew that her manager would be picking up the message she'd left her right about now: *Helen, this is Marcy. I'm taking the next three weeks off. Please cancel my appointments and have Anna reschedule. Thank you.*

Helen Dunbar would not be a happy camper.

At the insistent ringing, Marcy sighed. *Just get it over with,* she told herself. She knew she'd only prolong the inevitable if she didn't. Pulling the phone out of her navy-blue blazer pocket, she took a deep breath, then pushed the green button.

"Hello, Helen."

"Marcy, honey," Helen said, out of breath. "I got your message, and I'm on my way over to your place. We'll have some coffee and talk."

"There's nothing to talk about." Marcy could picture her manager now, dragging a brush through her cropped red hair, meticulously scanning her day planner and mentally reviewing the day's events, all while she talked on her speakerphone. "And there's no point in coming over. I'm not home."

"What do you mean, you're not home? Where are you?"

Marcy stared out the train window again, noticed a

hawk soaring over the plains. The magnificent sight stirred something in her blood, gave her courage. "I'm gone."

"Gone? What do you mean, gone? You can't be gone," Helen insisted. "We have an editorial meeting at one-thirty today to go over the November issue. We still have to discuss the article on creating a vintage table runner from grandma's linens, plus we need a new and creative way to stuff a turkey."

Marcy had a suggestion, but twenty-six years of manners and etiquette kept her from saying it. "Helen, I told you, I'm gone. I've left Los Angeles. In fact, I've left California."

"You what!"

There was a crash at the other end of the line, then Helen's muttered cursing about coffee on a new suit.

"I told you I needed some time off this month." Marcy pulled the bridal-shower party and wedding invitations from her canvas tote bag and laid them on her lap. "I'm taking it."

"Marcy—" Helen sighed patiently "—honey, we talked about this and agreed this isn't the time. You have an interview with *Stylish Homes* on Wednesday, a meeting on Thursday with the topics coordinator for the premiere of your TV show, then a celebrity charity luncheon at the Ritz-Carlton on Friday."

The thought of endless meetings, long hectic days and hurrying from one event to the next had Marcy instinctively reaching into her purse for an antacid.

She stared at the small, tin pillbox in her palm, tossed

it back into her purse, then reached for her emergency bag of chocolate-covered cherries instead. Sugar might not calm her nerves, she realized, but it would certainly make her feel better. "*We* didn't agree this was a bad time, Helen. You agreed."

"Marcy, we need you," Helen said firmly. "We'll find a better time and then I promise you can—"

"No."

There. She'd said it. She'd actually said *no*. Amazingly, the sky didn't spit lightning and the train hadn't derailed. Helen, on the other hand, had apparently been stunned into silence.

"No?" Helen said quietly after a long moment. "What do you mean, 'no'?"

"I mean no." The breath Marcy had been holding rushed out. "I'm not coming back."

After another long pause, Helen said hesitantly, "Marcy, honey, are you feeling okay?"

"Helen." Marcy struggled to keep her voice even and firm. "Last month I asked you not to schedule the next three weeks for me."

"Sweetie, I didn't think you were really serious, and you never were clear why you wanted so much—"

"And the month before that," Marcy interrupted, "I asked you not to schedule the same three weeks."

"But opportunities keep sprouting up like daisies. How can I not pick them?" Helen's voice softened. "Honey, I know it's been a grueling pace for the past four years. But it's paying off now. *Life With Marcy Pru-*

itt has quadrupled subscriptions, your Life and Home how-to column is syndicated, your last book hit the *Times* nonfiction list and your cable show is starting up in five weeks. You're practically a household name. Sweetie, there are a lot of people counting on you. There'll be time later to take off. I promise. Right now, we need you."

Marcy closed her eyes, felt the gentle rocking of the train underneath her. Maybe she was being selfish. Wanting time to herself, especially when everyone around her was working so hard, too. She didn't want to let anyone down. Didn't want to disappoint them.

And three weeks was a long time.

Marcy looked at the invitations again. Clair Beauchamp had been the only person in Marcy's life who had gone out of her way to make friends with the girl who didn't fit in. A painfully shy girl who wore horn-rimmed glasses and a simple, chin-length haircut.

How ironic it was that what had made her so different when she was growing up, was now her trademark.

Clair had asked her to be her maid of honor and she had said yes. She would *not* change her mind. Tucking the invitations back into her bag, Marcy straightened her shoulders. "I've left extensive notes and the project files with Anna. She knows them as well as I do, probably better. She can sit in for me until I get back."

Helen gasped. "You want your personal assistant to run your company! For God's sake, please tell me you aren't serious."

"I'm very serious. Anna has been with us for two

years now. She's more than capable. You'd know that if you'd give her a chance."

Marcy thought it best not to mention that Anna was also the only person who knew where she was going and why. If Helen had known, Marcy knew she'd never have been able to pull this off.

"Marcy, look, I know she's a good kid." Helen's voice turned frantic. "And I admit, she's a hard worker, too, but—"

"Sorry—" Marcy ran her fingertips back and forth over the cell-phone receiver "—you're breaking up. Gotta go."

"Marcy, no, please, listen to me, there's something you don't know. Something I should have told you. We need to talk in person. Just tell me where you—"

As if I'd fall for that, Marcy thought. Still, afraid she might weaken, she turned her phone off and slipped it back into the pocket of her blazer.

For the past four years, every aspect of her life had been carefully orchestrated. Meetings, TV appearances, more meetings, book tours, radio shows, fund-raising events. More meetings. She still loved her work as much as she always had, but in those four years, she hadn't taken one day for herself that wasn't connected to business in some way.

She was taking it now.

Nervous, but excited, Marcy folded her hands neatly on her lap, then looked out the train window and smiled.

* * *

Evan Carver stood in front of the floor-to-ceiling of-fice window and stared down at the Olympic-size swim-ming pool. The heat had brought out an interesting array of hotel guests today. On the east side of the pool three elderly men in Hawaiian shirts and cowboy hats played pinochle under the shade of a blue-striped um-brella. On the west side, a very pregnant brunette herded two little blond girls toward the shallow end, away from a group of teenage boys playing an enthusiastic game of volleyball in the deep end of the pool.

And finally, stretched out in lounge chairs on the south side of the pool, lay an entire row of sun-kissed, bikini-clad females.

Evan smiled.

He was single, between construction projects for the next three weeks and staying at a hotel with a conven-tion of swimsuit models.

Life couldn't possibly get any better.

"That's odd, she's not answering her cell phone."

"Hmm?" Evan glanced over his shoulder at his brother's fiancé. She sat at her sleek, cherrywood-and-glass desk, looking more like one of the models at the pool than the owner of an upscale hotel. Her suit jacket was the same deep blue as her eyes, her shoulder-length dark hair almost as black as her knee-length skirt. And while he could appreciate her fine, feminine qualities, Evan already thought of Clair Beauchamp as the sister he'd never had. "Who's not answering her phone?"

Frowning, Clair replaced the receiver in its cradle. "Marcy. All I'm getting is her voice mail."

Oh, right. Marcy. Clair had mentioned her maid of honor was coming into town today for the bridal shower tomorrow, then staying until the wedding. "Maybe she turned it off," he suggested.

"Marcy never turns her phone off."

"Out of range?"

"She shouldn't be." Clair glanced at the crystal-framed clock on her desk, then picked up her phone and pushed redial. "She's taking a train in from L.A. and I'd hoped to reach her before she gets to the station. I told her last night I'd be picking her up, but the editor in chief of *Texas Travel* showed up two days early and wants a tour of the hotel by yours truly."

"I'll pick her up for you," Evan said absently as he watched one of the boys in the pool bounce a wet beach ball on the stomach of a well-endowed blonde. *Smart kid,* Evan thought with a smile.

"I appreciate the offer." Sighing, Clair hung up the phone. "But it's really not necessary. I can send a hotel car."

"It's no problem." To the delight of every male within eyesight, the blonde stood and strolled to the edge of the pool, then with great flourish tossed the ball back. "Besides, didn't I tell Jacob I'd watch over things until he gets back from Philadelphia tomorrow?"

"He's in *Boston.*" Clair rose from her desk, then moved beside Evan and stared down at the pool. "I'm glad to see you take the job so seriously," she said, arching one eyebrow. "Maybe I *should* send a hotel car."

Turning from the window, he grinned at her. "What time is her train getting in?"

"Eleven-fifteen," Clair said hesitantly. "Are you sure you don't mind?"

"Just tell me what she looks like and I'm on my way."

Clair moved back to her desk, then picked up a magazine and handed it to him. "Here."

Life With Marcy Pruitt?

The cover of the magazine depicted the familiar brunette with black, horn-rimmed glasses sitting in a field of lavender. Her dress was lavender, as was the bouquet of flowers she held. The title read, "Lavender Fields Forever."

When Clair had said her friend's name was Marcy, it had never occurred to Evan she'd meant *that* Marcy. "Marcy Pruitt is your maid of honor?"

"You've heard of her?"

"Sure." Evan flipped through the articles in the magazine: making place cards from scraps of wallpaper; preparing an elegant dinner in less than thirty minutes; a master-bedroom makeover. "Didn't she write a book?"

Clair nodded. "Two books. *The Easy Life With Marcy Pruitt,* and *The Ultimate Easy Life With Marcy Pruitt.* How-to tips for the average homemaker. She's made quite a name for herself since our college days."

"You can say that again." Evan glanced at the cover again. She was kind of cute, he thought, in a quirky, homespun kind of way. "So is she single?"

Clair plucked the magazine away. "Yes, she's single, but trust me, she's not your type."

He winked at her. "Darlin', every woman's my type."

"Maybe I shouldn't trust you with her," Clair said, arching her eyebrow.

"Me?" Evan placed a hand over his heart. "I'm harmless."

"Of all the things you aren't, Evan Carver, it's harmless." But she smiled as she said it. "Also, we're keeping Marcy's trip here as quiet as possible, so she's going to be traveling incognito. Look for a big, white hat."

"That's incognito?"

"For Marcy it is." Clair pulled a card key out of her jacket pocket. "I'm putting her in the suite across from yours. Think you can behave?"

He gave her a crooked smile. "I'll manage to control myself."

"That's what your brother told me when I first met him." Clair waved her engagement ring at Evan. "Now look at us."

"Don't worry." Evan backed up as if the ring was made of kryptonite. "I'll deliver your friend safe and sound."

And right after he did—Evan glanced out the office window again—he intended to hightail it straight down to the pool.

* * *

At precisely eleven-fifteen, Marcy stepped off the train with the other passengers. It felt as presumptuous as it did ridiculous to wear the oversize, wide-brimmed hat and take off her glasses, but she preferred to err on the side of caution. Though the odds of anyone paying her any mind at the train depot were very slim—which was exactly the reason she'd chosen a train instead flying—she wasn't willing to push her luck or jeopardize her newfound freedom.

Suitcase in hand, she skirted a group of giggling adolescent girls wearing bright blue T-shirts that read CAMP WINNEMONKA. Based on all their energy and excitement, Marcy assumed the girls were on their way to camp, not returning.

Stepping to the side, Marcy set her suitcase down. No sign of Clair, but over the heads of the people hurrying through the station, Marcy couldn't help but notice a dark-haired man who stood several inches above most of the people in the depot. Arms folded over his broad chest, he was watching the passengers who were still pouring off the train.

Heavens.

Marcy knew very little—okay, she knew nothing—about men, but her lack of experience certainly didn't prevent her from appreciating a fine male specimen when she saw one. She *was* on a vacation, after all, so why shouldn't she enjoy the scenery? And anyway, it wasn't as if he'd notice her. Men who looked like that rarely gave her more than a cursory glance.

He stood like a rock in the swiftly moving stream of people. Six foot three, she thought, maybe taller. Rugged was the best word to describe the man, though handsome was certainly a close second. Based on his tanned face and muscled arms, she decided he probably worked outdoors. Square jaw. Strong chin. Large hands. Hair dark and thick, slightly wavy on the ends, skimmed the collar of his black T-shirt.

His eyes—brown?—narrowed slightly, and Marcy followed his gaze, noticed an attractive redhead stepping off the train. The woman smiled at the man and when he smiled back, Marcy felt her pulse skip. If she'd thought him handsome before, well, when he smiled, he was downright lethal.

You are one lucky woman, Marcy thought with a sigh.

But then, surprisingly, after the redhead hesitated a moment, she walked the other way. Curious, Marcy couldn't pull her gaze from the man, wanting to know who he was waiting for.

A slender blonde stepped off the train, definitely a possibility, Marcy thought, but she was greeted by two little girls and a man. Then a pretty brunette wearing a halter top and tight capris appeared. That *had* to be the one, and Marcy glanced back at the man to see his reaction.

"Excuse me."

Marcy jumped at the unexpected touch on her arm. Two women, fortyish, both wearing CAMP WIN-NEMONKA CAMP COUNSELOR T-shirts, stood beside her.

"Aren't you Marcy Pruitt?" the one with short, curly brown hair asked.

Marcy's stomach dropped. "Me?"

Not exactly a lie, but not an admission, either.

"I told you it wasn't her, Alice." The second woman, a pencil-thin platinum blonde, squinted and leaned in closer. "She doesn't look anything like her."

"Oh, for heaven's sake, Betty Lou." Exasperated, Alice shook her head. "She looks exactly like her. Put your glasses on."

"I don't need my glasses," the blonde argued. "It's not her."

"It is so." Alice looked back at Marcy and smiled. "Your article last month on homemade greeting cards was brilliant. Who would have ever thought to use old buttons and scraps of ribbon like that?"

"She's too skinny," Betty Lou insisted. "And too tall."

Alice rolled her eyes, then put a hand beside her mouth and whispered, "Don't mind Betty Lou. She just likes to be contrary."

"I'm not deaf, you know," Betty Lou harrumphed, then folded her arms and looked Marcy up and down. "I'm telling you it's not her."

"Marcy." Alice sighed. "Will you please tell my friend I'm right?"

If there was one thing that Marcy couldn't do well at all, it was lie. But if she told them the truth, she might as well go back to Los Angeles now. Her throat tightened, and she looked from one woman to the other. "I, well—"

"Darling. There you are."

At the sound of a deep male voice, Marcy turned. And froze.

The man she'd been staring at was now standing directly behind her, smiling down at *her.*

Had he just called her *darling?* Obviously he'd mistaken her for someone else, but before she could correct him, he pulled her into his arms. "I've been looking everywhere for you."

Marcy was too shocked to react, let alone speak. When he dropped his mouth down on hers, her heart slammed against her ribs. He tightened his hold on her and the feel of his chest against hers was like pressing against a brick wall.

Then he slid his mouth across her cheek and whispered in her ear, "Clair sent me."

His warm breath sent shivers up her spine. It took a moment for the words to make sense. *Clair sent me.* "Clair?"

"Clair. You know, your friend."

Wondering if he might have made a mistake, Evan lifted his head and stared at the woman. He supposed she did look a little different from the pictures he'd seen in her magazine. Not only because she wasn't wearing her renowned glasses, but something about her face looked softer, and her eyes, though wide as a frightened doe's, were the color of spring sage. He couldn't see her hair because of the ridiculous hat she had on, but based on the light brown bangs skimming the top of her eyebrows, he was fairly certain he had the right woman.

Evan dropped Marcy back to the ground, then slid an arm around her waist. "Who are your friends, darling?"

"They—" Marcy's voice cracked "—they think I'm Marcy Pruitt."

"Alice does," the blonde said. "I don't."

"Be quiet, Betty Lou." Alice narrowed her eyes and stared at Marcy. "She looks just like her."

"My wife gets that all the time." Evan laughed and yanked Marcy closer. "She can't hardly go anywhere someone doesn't ask for her autograph. Isn't that right, sugarplum?"

"I—ah." Marcy nodded. "It happens sometimes."

"What did I tell you?" Betty Lou crossed her arms and smiled at Alice. "Marcy isn't married. So now who's contrary?"

"I swear you could be her twin sister," Alice said, shaking her head. "It's amazing."

"You'll have to excuse us now, ladies." Evan picked up Marcy's suitcase, then winked at the women. "But I'd like to get my wife home and give her a proper hello, if you don't mind."

Betty Lou grinned and took hold of Alice's arm. "We don't mind at all. Sorry we bothered you."

Even as she was being dragged away, Alice kept staring.

For good measure, Evan squeezed Marcy again, then spun her around and headed in the opposite direction through the thinning crowd. "Well, that was close, though I'm not sure we convinced Alice and she just might—"

"Wait." Marcy yanked on his arm. *"Wait!"*

"What?" He stopped so abruptly she had to grab her hat to keep it from flying off her head.

"Who *are* you?"

"Evan." He glanced back to see if anyone was watching them, then pulled her around a corner and into a hallway that led to a lost-baggage claim office. "Evan Carver."

"Carver?" Her forehead furrowed, then lifted with recognition. "Jacob's brother?"

"The one and only." He grinned at her. "Clair tried to call your cell phone to give you a heads up, but you didn't answer."

"I turned it off." Nibbling her bottom lip, she studied him carefully.

"Clair had an unexpected meeting. If you're nervous about me driving you back to the Four Winds, you can call Clair's office and—"

"I'm not nervous." She pulled her arm away and straightened her shoulders. "You just caught me off guard. It's not every day a strange man kisses me and calls me his sugarplum."

"Sorry 'bout that." He grinned at her. "Clair told me you wanted to keep your trip quiet. When I saw those two women with you, I was trying to help."

"Actually, you did help," she said, then shoved her

hands into the pockets of her blazer. "I—I'm sorry. I don't mean to appear ungrateful."

The flush on the woman's cheeks brightened her face and made the green in her eyes appear darker. He realized he'd surprised her, but shoot, that little peck could hardly be considered a kiss.

She *had* tasted good, though, now that he thought about it. Like cherry—and chocolate, too. And her lips had been amazingly soft.

When a man and woman walked around the corner and glanced at Marcy, Evan moved in closer to shield her from their view. He waited until they moved past, then straightened.

"Shall we get the rest of your luggage?" he asked.

She glanced at the bag he already held. "That's all I have."

He furrowed his forehead. "You've only got one suitcase for three weeks?"

"Packing is really about making decisions on what you really do or don't need and sticking to a list." She shifted the canvas tote higher on her shoulder. "Lightweight garments that mix and match and don't wrinkle, two pairs of shoes, one pair of sandals, travel toiletries and a hat."

"Sounds like you wrote the book."

"Just a short article in last month's travel section."

"Really." Apparently, she hadn't realized he'd been teasing her. It seemed that Miss Marcy Pruitt was wound a little tight. "So have you written any articles on how to escape from a crowded train station without being seen?"

"That's scheduled for the January issue. I'm still researching that one."

For a split second, he thought she was being serious, but then he saw the corner of her mouth twitch. So the woman did have a sense of humor, after all. That was good, especially since he'd be spending the next thirty-five minutes in the car with her.

Grinning, he took her arm. "Ready to make a run for it, Miss Pruitt?"

"Ready when you are, Mr. Carver." She pulled her hat lower, then slipped her glasses back on. "Lead the way."

Two

Dear Marcy,
I am one of your biggest fans. (I tried your recipe
for chocolate cake in the February issue and loved
it!) In your interviews, you say you are shy, but
on television, you always appear so confident and
relaxed. What is your secret?
Linda from Kansas City

Suitcase in the trunk and hat folded in her canvas tote,
Marcy watched Evan pull out of the train station and ac-
celerate the shiny black luxury sedan smoothly onto the
open highway. She breathed in the scent of new car, then
slid her hand over the butter-soft leather seat. A glance
at the digital readout on the rearview mirror told her that
the interior of the sedan was a comfortable seventy-four
degrees, even though the temperature outside was a
scorching one hundred.

Somehow the polished, elegant car didn't quite suit

the man, she thought. With his large, callused hands, broad shoulders and faded blue jeans, she could easily picture Clair's future brother-in-law behind the wheel of a pickup or a Jeep or even a Hummer. Something masculine and tough that could drive off the road and splash through mud, rumble over huge boulders or tear through thick terrain.

"Something wrong?" Evan asked.

"Wrong?" She looked at him, realized that she had leaned forward to run her fingers over the grain of the mahogany dashboard. Self-conscious, she snatched her hand away and straightened. Touching things, needing to know the feel and texture or analyze how it was made had become so second nature to her, she rarely knew when she was doing it.

"No, nothing's wrong." She folded her hands in her lap. "I was just admiring your car."

"Not mine, the hotel's," he said, turning his attention back to the road. "For some strange reason, Clair thought you'd be more comfortable in this than my pickup. You women from California have something against trucks?"

"No, of course not. I wouldn't have minded at all. And I'm not really from California. I was actually born in Burbridge, Ohio, it's just a small town outside of— oh." She saw one corner of his mouth curve. "You're kidding."

He grinned. "Sorry. Couldn't resist. Actually, this car's fun to drive. Even at ninety, she still purrs like a kitten."

Ninety? Marcy swallowed hard. She didn't think she'd ever gotten her little Camry over sixty-five. When Evan suddenly zipped into the left lane to pass a truck and horse trailer, she grabbed onto the seat belt. He sped up, then zipped back into the right lane and slowed down again.

Good heavens! The man certainly liked to drive fast.

It took a moment for her stomach to slide back down from her throat.

"Music?"

"What?" She loosened her grip on the seat belt. "Oh, sure. Whatever you like."

He settled on a Rolling Stones song, and while Mick Jagger sang about moving it to the left and then the right, Marcy watched the passing countryside. The open space amazed her. Big, white farmhouses and tall, red barns. Pastures, horses and cows. A man riding a large green tractor in a field waved as they drove by. They were as blissfully far from the city as a person could get.

"Feels good to play hookey, doesn't it?"

Turning, she looked back at Evan, realized he'd been watching her. He had those kind of eyes. Dark and intense, not just intelligent, but…observant. Eyes that didn't just look *at* you like most people's, but eyes that looked *inside*. Suddenly the car felt smaller, the space between them shorter. "Hookey?"

"You know, sneaking away from work, hiding out from all those exciting meetings."

"Oh. Right." She looked back at the road ahead of them, watched the heat curling up off the asphalt. "I don't think it's quite sunk in just yet. I keep expecting Helen to jump up out of the back seat or suddenly drive alongside of us."

"Helen?"

"My manager. She's not very happy with me right now."

"Because you're taking a few days off?" Evan asked. When he sped up and passed a semi-truck, Marcy held her breath.

"Three weeks is a lot more than a few days." She slowly released her breath when they were back in their own lane again. "To Helen, that's a lifetime. On top of that, I wouldn't tell her where I was going. It will drive her crazy."

"It's good to drive people crazy once in a while. Keeps them on their toes."

Marcy imagined that Evan kept lots of people on their toes, most of them female. Since that kiss he'd given her at the bus station, she'd been more than a little off balance.

Not that she considered it a real *kiss,* in a man-woman sense of the word. But nevertheless, as ridiculous as it was, the unexpected brush of his lips on hers had made it difficult for her to concentrate on anything else.

Good grief, she *really* needed to start dating more. Well, actually, she just needed to start dating, period. Working 24/7 these past four years had definitely taken its toll on her personal life. The fact was, she had no personal life. And now that she'd decided to get one, conse-quences be damned, she wasn't sure what to do with it.

What she did know, was that it was time to stop act-ing like a timid child. In new situations, she had always been a little nervous. Even now, every time she spoke in public or did guest spots on TV, her knees shook. And just thinking about her upcoming television show sent a shot of adrenaline rushing through the pit of her stom-ach.

The only way she'd survived these past four years in the limelight were the techniques she'd learned to calm her nerves. Looking over at Evan, it seemed as if there was no time like the present to apply a few of those tech-niques—although the one about seeing your audience naked didn't seem like the best one to use at the mo-ment.

Breathe. Slowly…deeply, release. Three times.

Visualize my peaceful place. Toes in the sand, on an empty beach.

Concentrate. Think about what needs to be done and how to do it.

"You okay over there?" Evan asked.

"Fine." Calmer now, she slowly released her third breath and looked at Evan. "Clair told me you own a construction company. What do you build?"

"Custom homes, mostly." He turned off the highway onto a picturesque, tree-lined road and slowed the car's speed. "I buy ten- to fifteen-acre parcels around the state and build five to seven houses on them."

"Why so few?" In L.A., Marcy thought, there would probably be closer to thirty or forty houses on that amount of land.

"Because I believe in space, for one thing," Evan said. "For another, if I'm in one place or with the same project for more than a few months, I get antsy."

"Antsy to get back home?"

He shook his head. "Antsy to move on. My 'home' is a twenty-eight-foot fifth wheel that goes with me."

"You build houses, but you live in a trailer?" she said in amazement.

"I'm not home enough to mow lawns or clean gutters," he said with a shrug. "What about you? What kind of house does Marcy Pruitt live in? Wait, let me guess—country cottage with a white picket fence and rose gardens?"

"More like Canyon Cottage, picket fence and bare dirt." She'd fallen in love the minute she'd laid eyes on the house nestled beside a creek off the Malibu coast. "I just moved in six months ago and it still needs a lot of work."

"Will it be in 'Marcy's Makeover' column?"

Surprised, she looked at him. Marcy's Makeover was the most popular monthly feature article in her magazine. Sometimes they took a single room in a house, sometimes they took an entire house, then gave it a new look. "You've read my magazine?"

"I glanced through a copy in Clair's office. The one where you're sitting in a field of lavender."

"Oh." She always felt uncomfortable about being on the cover, but her publisher insisted she appear on at least four of the twelve monthly issues. "I've never done a makeover on a trailer. How about you let me do one on yours?"

He shot her a you've-got-to-be-kidding-me look.

"I promise I won't use pink or feathers," she reassured him, but could have sworn he paled at the very thought.

"Thanks, but no thanks. Here we are, Miss Pruitt." He passed a gas station connected to a motor lodge and café, then turned left off the two-lane road. "Welcome to Wolf River."

Small-town America was alive and well, Marcy noted as they drove down Main Street. The storefronts were brick and shiny glass, the stores themselves offered a variety of just about anything a person might need, including a wide range of restaurants. Shoppers strolled along freshly swept sidewalks, in no apparent hurry to get wherever it was they were going.

Clearly, the pace was slower here and the traffic was light. By Los Angeles standards, she thought, it was deserted. There were more pickup trucks than any other vehicle on the streets, and only two stoplights that she could see, but when they drove past a side street, she spotted a multiplex theater and two popular fast-food chains. Based on the construction taking place off the main drive into town, it appeared that Wolf River was growing by leaps and bounds.

But the newest and one of the largest additions to the town, Marcy knew, was the Four Winds Hotel. It sat at the east end of town—not especially large by city standards, but for Wolf River, the twelve-story hotel stood like a skyscraper. Under a wide, spreading portico, beside a pair of tall, glass entry doors, a trio of life-size bronze horses seemed to be racing through a water fountain. Huge brass planters of white and purple petunias, cooled by an overhead mist system, lined the curb where uniformed bellmen greeted guests and handled luggage.

"It's beautiful," she murmured.

The first time he'd seen it, the elegance of the Four Winds had surprised him, too, especially compared to the size of Wolf River. "Wait till you see the inside. It'll knock your socks off."

He pulled the car around to a side entrance with an iron gate and pressed a remote clipped to the visor. The gate opened and he drove through, then parked in an underground area reserved for the hotel guests staying on the top floor.

"There's a private elevator that will take us to the suites." He slid out of the front seat and came around to open Marcy's door. "I'd take you on a tour, but this is Clair's baby and I have the feeling she'd like the honors."

"I can't wait to see it." She followed him to the elevator after he plucked her suitcase out of the trunk. "It's just so hard to believe that only a few months ago she was still in Charleston and was going to marry Oliver and—" She stopped and bit her lip. "Sorry. I shouldn't have mentioned that."

"It's hardly a secret, Marcy." Evan held the elevator door open. A Beatles' instrumental, "Love Me Do," played softly on the overhead speakers. "Did you know him?"

"I met him a few times when he came to see Clair at Radcliffe, but there were no warm fuzzies between us. He didn't approve of Clair's friendship with me."

Frowning, Evan pushed the button for the top floor. "What do you mean, 'he didn't approve'?"

"To help pay my way through school, I not only did some light housekeeping, I started catering for the faculty parties," she said. "One time I overheard Oliver tell Clair it didn't look good for her to be roommates with the girl who cleaned houses and prepared food for the teachers."

"What an ass," Evan muttered under his breath.

Marcy smiled. "I think it was the only time I ever saw Clair angry. She told him if he couldn't be nice to me, then she couldn't marry him. After that, Oliver was so polite and so friendly every time he saw me, it was all I could do not to laugh. I know it killed him, which only made me want to laugh all the more."

"Sounds like we're both happy she didn't marry the jerk," Evan said.

The elevator doors slid open silently and they stepped into a small lobby with a polished black-marble floor and sparkling crystal chandelier. Against one wall sat a

cranberry-colored suede sofa and two tapestry arm-
chairs, and against the opposite wall was an antique
sideboard with coffee-and-tea service, plus fresh-baked
goods.

Her suite was at the end of the hall, and when Evan
opened the door for her, the scent of flowers drifted
from the room. On the entry table, a huge bouquet of
white roses filled a cut-crystal vase.

"Oh, they're beautiful." Marcy rushed to the roses
and stuck her nose in them.

There it was again, Evan thought as he watched her
breathe in the scent of the flowers. That uninhibited rush
of excitement, the softening of her voice. He liked this
side of Marcy Pruitt, he decided as he watched her slide
the tips of her long, slender fingers over the rose petals.

Her skin had felt like that, he remembered. And her lips.

Realizing his thoughts were taking him in an odd direction, he cleared his throat. "Bedroom?"

"Excuse me?" Her head swung around.

"Your suitcase. Shall I put it in the bedroom?"

"Oh. No, thank you." She turned from the flowers
and moved toward him, her hand outstretched. "I'll take
it from here. You've already done more than enough and
I really—"

She stopped suddenly and sniffed the air. Her eyes
widened. "Hamburgers," she said, her voice a bit
breathless.

"What?"

"Hamburgers," she repeated, then spun on the heels

of her navy-blue flats and hurried into the living area of the suite.

Intrigued, he followed her, watched her lift a shiny silver lid off a tray sitting on a food cart. "Oh, look at this," she said with a laugh.

Evan set the suitcase down and moved beside Marcy. "Yep. Hamburgers, all right."

A pile of hamburgers, actually. Surrounded by a moat of thin, tiny French fries. Around the outside edges were little silver bowls of condiments, everything from ketchup to pickles to chili and cheese.

"Now that's room service," he said with admiration. "So what gives?"

"This is Clair's way of saying hello," Marcy said, then laughed again when she lifted the lid off a second plate that contained a huge slice of dark chocolate cake, a small, napkin-lined basket of candy bars and a can of spray whipped cream chilling in a crystal bowl of ice. "In college, Clair was a health nut and always on a diet of some kind, even though she never needed to be. But I, on the other hand, was a food junkie. What you're looking at here was my favorite four-course meal."

"My kind of woman." Evan stared in awe at the feast on the table. "Maybe we should get married."

"I'm a little busy right now." Smiling, she dipped her finger in the chocolate icing. "Ask me again later." Evan swallowed the sudden lump in his throat when Marcy licked the chocolate icing off her finger, then closed her eyes on a soft moan.

"Would you like to join me?" she asked, opening her eyes.

He had to wait a moment for his pulse to steady, reminding himself they were talking about food here and nothing else. There had to be something seriously wrong with his hormones, he decided, mentally shaking his head, and blamed the unexpected jolt of lust on the mouthwatering display of food.

Smiling, he politely pulled a chair out for her and gestured for her to sit. "I thought you'd never ask."

Seated at the table, her napkin neatly on her lap, Marcy watched in fascination while Evan methodically assembled his hamburger. For her own, she'd gone with a little mayonnaise, lettuce and a tomato, while the only condiments Evan seemed to have bypassed were the mustard and pickles.

Everything about the man seemed bigger than life, she thought. His size, his personality, his looks.

And definitely his masculinity.

She decided conversation would distract her from thinking so much. "Clair told me you and Jacob were raised in New Jersey. What brought you to Texas?"

He reached for the mustard and dropped a dollop on his open bun. "U.T."

"University of Texas?"

"Six years." He gave her a goofy grin. "Got me a master's in science."

She raised an eyebrow at that and handed him the pickles. "But you ended up in construction."

"I hated working indoors. Thanks." He took the pickles and spread a layer on his bun. "I spent a summer as a carpenter and found out I not only liked working with my hands, I was good at it."

She studied his hands now as he finished building his mansion of a hamburger. They were large and had a rough appearance. His fingers were long, his nails cut short. It was easy to picture him holding a hammer or a saw, but when her imagination took her further and she pictured him without a shirt, his tanned face and broad chest covered with sweat, she quickly blinked the image out of her mind.

Turning her attention back to his hamburger, she watched him take a bite of his creation, then frown.

"Something wrong?" she asked.

He looked at the condiment bowls. "Needs something."

"More ketchup?"

"Amateur." He dumped a few French fries on his burger and took another bite. "Much better."

"French fries on your hamburger?" She stared at him in amazement. "Really?"

"Bet that's not in any of your recipes." He held out his hamburger to her. "Try it."

"No thanks." Admittedly, she *was* curious, but taking a bite of his food seemed like such a personal thing to do. "I'm fine."

"One little bite." He waved it under her nose. "Come on, sugarplum. I dare you."

Sugarplum. She frowned at him. Well, a dare *was* a dare, she thought. And it *did* smell good. She leaned forward and nipped off a tiny bite.

"You call that a bite?" He shook his head. "Come on, show me the stuff Marcy Pruitt's made of."

With a sigh, she put her hands on his, then took a healthy sample of his concoction. Out of habit, she closed her eyes and focused on identifying every taste.

"Well?" he asked.

"Sweet." She licked her lips. "Definitely salty." She chewed slowly, letting her taste buds explore. "Interesting."

Somewhere between Marcy's murmur of "sweet" and "salty," Evan's mouth turned dry as a midsummer's creek. With her eyes closed and her mouth slightly pursed, Marcy's face had taken on an appearance of sheer pleasure and absolute delight. But it was the slow slide of her tongue over her lips that had pushed him over the line of just messing around to something completely different.

He couldn't take his eyes off her lips.

She had the most amazing mouth. Wide, full, with corners turned upward. When the tip of her tongue swept over her bottom lip again, he felt a jolt of pure, unadulterated lust.

This was Marcy Pruitt, for crying out loud, he told himself. And Clair's friend, on top of it. He had no business thinking what he was thinking.

When she made a small sound of pleasure deep in

her throat, sweat broke out on his forehead. He yanked the hamburger back, then hunkered down in his chair and took a bite, trying not to think about the fact that her mouth had just touched the very spot he'd bite off.

Marcy opened her eyes and smiled. "I like it. Is it your secret recipe, or can I use it in my magazine?"

"It's all yours," he said as casually as he could muster. "Do whatever you like with it."

Her eyes narrowed thoughtfully. "I don't think I've done an article on hamburgers yet. It might be interesting."

He thought it would be a pretty short article. What was there to know? Meat, bun, lots of condiments.

"Knock, knock." Clair stuck her head in the door. "Anybody home?"

Evan watched Marcy's face light up when she saw Clair, who was already hurrying across the room, her arms spread. The women hugged each other and laughed.

"Did Evan find you all right?" Clair's words rushed out. "I guess he did, since you're here. Oh, I've missed you so much!"

Sniffing, Marcy pulled a tissue out of her pocket and dabbed at her eyes. "You look absolutely radiant. Being in love and buying a hotel obviously agrees with you."

"It does. And you—" Clair wiped at her own eyes. "Your own magazine and books and a syndicated column. It makes my head spin."

"I have a great group of people I work with," Marcy said. "I couldn't do any of it without them."

"You always were modest." Clair hugged her again. "But that's one of the reasons I love you. Oh, I can't wait for Jacob to meet you. He'll be back in town tomorrow morning, so you and I are having a slumber party tonight."

"Can I come, too?" Evan asked hopefully.

"Not a chance." Clair moved to Evan and kissed his cheek. "But thank you for picking Marcy up. Did you find her all right?"

"Big white hat." He grinned at Marcy. "And a crowd of adoring fans."

"Two is hardly a crowd," Marcy said, shaking her head. "And Evan managed to throw them off."

"Really?" Clair arched an eyebrow and looked at Evan. "How did you do that?"

He grinned at Marcy, who blushed. "I kissed her and said she was my wife."

Clair gasped. "You did what?"

"I had to do something," he said. "Alice and Betty Lou were closing in."

"Alice and Betty Lou?" Confused, Clair narrowed her eyes.

"Alice, actually. Betty Lou didn't think our girl here looked anything like Marcy Pruitt."

Jaw slack, Clair looked at Marcy. "He's kidding, right?"

"Actually, he's telling the truth," Marcy said. "Betty Lou thought I was too skinny and too tall to be Marcy Pruitt."

Dumbfounded, Clair looked from Evan to Marcy,

then just laughed and hugged Marcy again. "Sounds like we have a lot to catch up on. I've cleared my afternoon schedule so we can start right now."

"I can take a hint." Evan stood. "You guys have fun."

Marcy held out her hand. "Thank you for picking me up."

"No problem." Smiling, he took her fingers in his. "Anytime you need a ride or a husband, just let me know."

Her blush deepened. "I'll do that."

"So you want to tell me what happened?" Clair looked at Marcy after Evan closed the door behind him.

"What do you mean?"

"Did he really kiss you?"

"Only with the best of intentions," Marcy said, annoyed when the memory of that kiss made her lips tingle. "I assure you, he was much more interested in these hamburgers than me, which I haven't even thanked you for yet. A stroke of genius on your part, Miss Beauchamp."

"The kitchen thought it a little odd when I put the order in," Clair said with a grin. "But you've barely eaten anything. Sit down and eat while I talk your ear off about Jacob."

The love shining in Clair's eyes made Marcy's chest tighten. "He must be special. You never glowed when you were with Oliver."

"I came so close to making the worst mistake of my life." Pulling her pumps off, Clair sat cross-legged on the chair Evan had occupied. "If Jacob hadn't found me, I'd be Mrs. Oliver Hollingsworth right now."

When Marcy reached for a handful of fries and placed them neatly on her hamburger, Clair gave her a questioning glance. Marcy smiled. "Evan's idea."

"Watch out for any ideas from Evan," Clair warned. "He's got way too many."

"That's the last thing I need to worry about," she said. "Men don't look at me that way."

"You're a beautiful woman, Marcy," Clair said firmly. "If you weren't hiding behind big glasses and a haircut that covers most of your face, you'd be fighting off the men."

The very thought made her laugh. "I'm not hiding. This is just who I am. And even if I wanted to change, I really couldn't. People expect me to look and behave a certain way."

Clair sighed and shook her head. "Honey, if I can learn not to worry about people's expectations, then anybody can. There's a wild woman inside Marcy Pruitt," Clair said with a grin. "She's just waiting for you to let her loose."

A wild woman! Marcy shook her head at Clair's foolishness. But it felt good to be silly, she thought, to relax and laugh with an old friend.

"Enough about me," she said, still chuckling. "We were talking about you and Jacob, remember? Now start from the very beginning and don't leave out one single detail."

Three

Dear Marcy,
My fiancé and I are planning a summer wedding.
We would like to have the ceremony outdoors, but
worry about problems with the weather. What is
your opinion?
Tiffany and Chris in Woodland Hills

The details of Clair's story, Marcy soon found out,
were fascinating.

It would make an incredible movie. A car crash on
an icy road outside a small town. A father and mother
killed, but their three children survive: two boys, seven
and nine, one little girl, barely three. A greedy, hate-
driven uncle who separates the children and pays a cor-
rupt lawyer to illegally adopt the children out, none of
them knowing their siblings are alive. Twenty-three
years later, a cousin learns the truth and hires a private

investigator to find the children and reunite the family. Jacob was the private investigator. Clair was the little girl.

"And you found all this out two days before your wedding?" Marcy asked, still trying to absorb the enormity of Clair's story.

"I was having a last-minute fitting on my wedding dress," Clair said. "Jacob followed me when I came out of the shop. He told me that I had been born in Wolf River County, Texas, that my real name—my birth name—was Elizabeth Marie Blackhawk, and that I had two older brothers, Rand and Seth."

They'd settled comfortably on the white sectional sofa in the living room of the suite. Room service had come and gone with a basket of blueberry scones and a pot of fragrant peppermint tea. With their shoes off and their feet tucked under their legs, Marcy listened while Clair continued.

"It was so absurd, I didn't believe him at first. I thought he was a crazy person, or he'd made a huge mistake. How could my parents have lied to me like that?" Clair poured two cups of tea and handed one to Marcy. "But he had proof. Pictures, newspaper articles of the accident. A birth certificate. Even copies of the adoption papers signed by my parents." Clair stared at the steam rising off her tea. "It explained so much. I had parents who loved me, money, the best education. And yet I always had such a strong sense that something was missing in my life. That something wasn't quite right and I just didn't fit in."

Now *that* was a feeling Marcy could relate to. After

her own parents had died and she'd gone to live with her Aunt Hattie, Marcy had been the proverbial square peg. Her aunt, an eccentric widow with no children of her own, had never quite known what to do with her eight-year-old niece. On an intellectual level, Marcy understood why she was different from the other kids, but that certainly didn't make it any less painful. Didn't make it any less difficult.

But sitting here with Clair, Marcy thought, sharing tea and scones, this was easy. It didn't matter that they hadn't seen each other in a year or that they didn't even speak that often. The time dissolved and there was only then and only now.

"I'm sorry I wasn't there for you when all this happened," Marcy said with a sigh. "I've spent the past four years listening to other people tell me where to be and what to do for the good of my career. I'm finally learning how to say no."

"Good for you. Here's to that one little, but extremely powerful word." Clair tapped her cup lightly against Marcy's. "But it really was for the best you couldn't make it. I would have felt awful if you'd canceled a European book tour for my wedding, only to watch me run out of the church while the bridal march was playing."

"I actually do wish I could have been there to see that," Marcy said. "I can't imagine myself doing anything that brave."

Clair shook her head. "It certainly didn't feel brave at the time. But when I saw Jacob standing at the back of church and our eyes met, I knew I couldn't marry Oliver and live a lie. I walked right up to Jacob and asked him for a ride, and I haven't looked back since." Tears filled Clair's eyes. "For the first time in my life, everything feels right. Jacob, meeting my brothers, buying the Four Winds. And now having you here. Life is perfect."

"Don't make me cry, too." Swallowing back the thickness in her throat, Marcy squeezed Clair's hand. "I'm just so happy that you're happy. Jacob is lucky to have you."

"I'm the lucky one," Clair said, beaming. "But enough about me and Jacob for now. I want to hear about your magazine. And tell me—" Clair leaned closer "—do you really write all the answers to the questions in your lifestyle advice column yourself?"

Laughing, Marcy sipped her tea and settled back on the sofa. "Every last one."

It was a good morning for a swim. Air still fresh and slightly crisp, and at six-thirty, most of the hotel guests were still sleeping or in their rooms sipping their first cup of coffee. Except for the soft hum of the pool filter and the distant flutter of birds in a nearby tree, it was stone quiet.

Peeling his T-shirt off, Evan dove into the deep end and cut smoothly through the cool water. It seemed like a million years ago he'd been on the swim team in high school, even though it had only been—what? Twelve years. Damn. That *was* a million years ago.

He finished his first lap and moved into his second. He enjoyed the invigorating pump of blood through his system, fell easily into a rhythm and held it.

Out of habit, he always woke early. Working in construction, a man had to start his day at the crack of dawn to get a jump on the hot Texas sun. He enjoyed every aspect of his work, from the design element to swinging a hammer to digging trenches. He loved to start with nothing but a piece of dusty, weed-congested dirt, then build something that would stand the test of time. He'd finished up his last project just last week and already he was impatient for something to keep his hands and mind occupied.

Women, of course, were always his first choice to fill his spare time. While he was on a job, his day started too early and ended too late to give the opposite sex the attention they required. Which meant that he had a lot of time to make up for when he wasn't working.

Last night, he'd met a couple of the swimsuit models, Mandy and Suzanne, in the lounge downstairs. They'd invited him to a party they were throwing tonight in their suite, but with the bridal party for Jacob and Clair, he'd had to turn the women down.

Personally, he didn't think men belonged at a bridal shower, or anywhere near one, for that matter. But Clair had insisted that the party was for the bride *and* the groom, and that it was his sibling responsibility to attend.

With Jacob settling down, Evan figured his greatest sibling responsibility was to pick up the slack with all the single women, starting with Mandy and Suzanne. But since neither Clair nor Jacob would see it that way, he supposed the models would just have to party tonight without him.

A damn shame, he thought.

But Mandy and Suzanne weren't the only women on his mind this morning, Evan realized as he pushed off the side of the pool for his fourth lap. Strangely enough, he'd also been thinking about Marcy.

Before yesterday, he'd never given much thought to the woman one way or the other. Now that he'd met her, it seemed he couldn't quite get her out of his mind.

That funny, oversize hat. Her startled look when he'd kissed her at the train depot. The almost sexual manner in which she'd touched and smelled the roses Clair had sent. The expression of pure pleasure on her face when she'd tasted his hamburger.

He'd wanted to taste her lips at that moment. Wanted to lick the salty sweetness. He was thankful that Clair had walked in, or he just might have. He could only imagine he would have scared Marcy to death if he actually *had* kissed her. Not like the little peck he'd given her at the depot, but a real kiss.

I might still kiss her, he thought. A slow and easy kiss, nothing too suggestive. He didn't want to give her the wrong idea or scare her. He just wanted a little taste, that's all. Enough to satisfy his curiosity.

Or maybe he just needed another fifteen laps in the pool. Some physical exertion to burn up the excess energy he always had when he wasn't working. But then he thought about how soft Marcy's lips were, how smooth her skin had looked.

Better make it twenty-five, he told himself and pushed off the side of the pool again.

If Marcy had thought the outside of the Four Winds Hotel elegant, then the only word for the downstairs lobby was exquisite. Freshly polished black Italian-marble floors shone under huge iron-and-elk-horn chandeliers. Strategically placed antique European tables blended with rugged wood beams and adobe walls. In the main lobby, a giant bouquet of sunflowers and purple delphiniums graced an oval glass table. Sofas and easy chairs in shades of rich browns and deep reds invited guests to relax while strains of classical music mingled with the sound of water bubbling from a stone-wall fountain.

Casual sophistication, Marcy decided, following Clair on her early-morning round of the hotel. They'd already toured the well-equipped gym and spa, a lovely clothes boutique, a luxurious beauty salon and a spot-less, state-of-the art kitchen that serviced the two hotel restaurants. From wrapped chocolate mints to fresh coffee service by the registration desk, it appeared that no detail had been overlooked.

"You must be exhausted," Clair said when Marcy stopped to examine a bronze statue of a horse on a side table. "All that traveling, then I keep you up all night talking your ear off."

"I seem to recall doing my fair share of talking." The bronze was wonderful, by an artist she'd never heard of before. Marcy filed the name away. "And one o'clock is hardly all night."

"It is when you get up at five-thirty." Clair waved to a pretty brunette behind the registration desk. "And what good is a vacation if you can't sleep in?"

It was only six-thirty now, and except for staff, the hotel lobby was empty. It seemed to Marcy that it was the best time to see the hotel without needing to wear a hat. "I couldn't sleep anyway," she said truthfully. "I was too anxious to see your hotel. I absolutely love what you've done."

"My cousin Lucas designed and built the hotel as a tourist and conference center." Clair led Marcy down a hallway past the lobby elevators. "I just did some remodeling when I bought it from him. Olivia Cameron is the interior designer I've been working with for the past few months. She owns an antique store in town."

"I'd love to meet her," Marcy said. "Our upcoming January issue is going to be dedicated to small-town antique stores. Maybe we can include her."

"She'll be at the party tonight, you can meet her then." Clair paused to stare at a vase of flowers sitting on a granite-topped rosewood table. She turned the vase a centimeter, then moved on. "I want to show you my office, then we'll have breakfast."

Marcy followed Clair through double glass doors

that led back to the private lobby and set of elevators reserved for the executive staff and guests staying in the suites. The elevator doors opened and a man wearing a charcoal suit and silver tie stepped out. He was tall, his thick, dark hair short and neat. When he smiled at Clair, the corners of his startling deep blue eyes crinkled. "Miss Beauchamp." He nodded, then turned his gaze on Marcy. "Miss Pruitt. Welcome to the Four Winds."

"Sam Prescott is my general manager," Clair explained. "I told him you'd be staying with us. You can trust him and all the staff here to be discreet."

"A pleasure, Mr. Prescott."

"Sam," he said, taking the hand she offered. "And the pleasure is mine. If there's anything at all I can do to make your stay with us more comfortable, please don't hesitate to let me know."

"Thank you."

"Ladies." Sam held the elevator door open. "Enjoy your day."

After the elevator door closed again, Marcy looked at Clair and blurted out, "Good heavens, are *all* the men in this town handsome?"

Laughing, Clair pushed the third-floor button. "Wait till you meet my cousin and brothers. If they weren't taken, I'd fix you up."

Evan's not taken.

The thought popped into her head before Marcy could stop it, and she breathed a silent sigh of relief that she hadn't said it out loud.

She'd thought about him last night, just before she fell asleep. It embarrassed her a little to think about it now in the light of day. She'd never been one to overly engage in sexual fantasies. Not because she was a prude, but simply because she'd never met a man whom she'd been so attracted to, or a man who had…stimulated that line of thinking.

But lying in that big bed alone, on the soft sheets and firm mattress, she'd wondered what it would be like if he'd been there with her. Wondered what his muscles would feel like under her hands. What his skin would feel like. How it would taste.

That thought made her stomach flutter and her pulse quicken.

"You okay?" Clair held the elevator doors open, waiting for Marcy to step off.

"What? Oh, yes. Fine." Flustered, she hurried off the elevator. "It's just that I'm still in awe this is all yours."

"Me, too." Clair smiled and headed down the hallway. The carpet was plush royal-blue, the paintings on the walls nineteenth-century western artists. Clair opened a tall, pale oak door. "I couldn't think of a better way to start a new life and at the same time invest the inheritance I received from the Blackhawk estate. After you."

"Oh, Clair, I love this," Marcy said when she stepped inside the office. The room had a slightly more traditional look to it, with just a touch of vintage china and crystal ware on the mahogany bookshelves and desk. "It's wonderful."

"It's still a work in progress, but I'm getting there." Clair stepped to her desk and picked up the phone. "Just let me check my messages and we'll go down and eat."

Marcy moved to the floor-to-ceiling windows and stared down at the pool, then slipped off her glasses to watch a lone swimmer cut through the light fog rising off the water. A man, she realized. His strokes were sure and even and when he reached the pool's edge, he rose up a moment.

Marcy's pulse jumped.

It was Evan.

When he kicked off the edge again to continue another lap, she couldn't take her eyes off him. He moved across the pool in what seemed like an effortless burst of power, muscles rippling as he sliced through the water. Lord, he was a sight to behold! Long legs. Hard, wet body. It was enough to take a woman's breath away.

He moved across the pool again, paused, then placed his hands on the deck and swung himself out of the water. Water glistened on his tanned skin, and she couldn't help but admire the curves and angles of solid muscle and his flat, hard stomach. He dragged a hand through his wet hair, then reached for a towel. His navy-blue swim trunks clung to his body.

She leaned closer to the window, wishing she had a pair of binoculars.

"Ready?" Clair asked, hanging up the phone.

"What?" Marcy turned quickly on knees that felt loose. "Oh, sure."

But even as she walked away, even as she forced the image of Evan's half-naked, wet body from her mind, she heard a little voice whisper, *"Are you?"*

After he dressed, it took Evan a while to track Clair and Marcy down to a large, private patio off the main ballroom where they were having breakfast outdoors. Leaning against the doorjamb, he watched them drinking coffee and nibbling on pastries.

Women fascinated him. They were impossible to predict. Usually fickle. God knew he'd given up trying to understand them years ago. Now he simply enjoyed them. The way they moved, the way they smelled.

All those wonderful curves.

He looked at Marcy, tried to visualize her curves under the pink long-sleeved shirt and tailored slacks she had on. He knew she was slender, but she seemed to go out of her way to cover up the details.

Which only made him wonder all the more.

She was laughing at something Clair said, and the sound had an almost musical quality to it. He smiled, watched her lean close to Clair and whisper something, then they both laughed.

He knew he should walk away. Leave them to share their secrets and catch up on lost time.

But hey, they'd had all night to do that, hadn't they?

He pushed away from the doorjamb and moved across the patio. "Morning, ladies."

Marcy's smile froze when she looked up and met his gaze. It was almost visible, the defensive shield she raised with strangers. He wasn't certain if she was aware of her own self-defense system, but he certainly understood why she did it. It had to be a bitch, living her life like a mannequin in a store window. She probably couldn't even go out to eat without it being reported the next day what restaurant she'd gone to, who she'd been with, what she'd eaten.

I sure as hell couldn't live like that, Evan thought. But since he didn't have to, he had no reason to be concerned about it, either.

"Evan." Turning, Clair smiled at him. "Come join us."

"I don't want to intrude."

"Yes, you do." Clair poured him a cup of coffee. "You're bored to death with Jacob gone. Admit it."

"I'm never bored around pretty ladies." He looked at Marcy. "Morning, Miss Pruitt."

He felt a sense of accomplishment when the smile on her lips made it to her eyes. "Good morning, Mr. Carver."

"So formal," Clair teased. "And to think it was only yesterday you two were married."

"She left me," Evan said with a sigh, then eyed the basket of pastries on the table. "But one of those Danish and maybe some ham and eggs might ease the pain."

"I'll see what I can do about the latter." Clair lifted the basket and held it out to him. "As to the former, what would you like?"

Before he could decide, Evan was distracted when Marcy lifted her coffee cup to her smiling lips. Once again he found himself entranced with her mouth. *What would he like?* He could think of several things.

But since Clair was referring to breakfast, he decided on an apple Danish, then sat in the chair beside Marcy. "So when will Big Jake be here?"

"Anytime now." Clair glanced at her wristwatch. "But he's mine for the morning. We have an appointment with the photographer. You can have him this afternoon when you go for your tux fittings."

Evan frowned. Damn. He hated those fitting things. Twice before—his high-school prom and his foreman's wedding three years ago—he'd been subjected to what he considered the male equivalent of a nineteenth-century corset. "You know, it's still not too late to fly to Vegas," he suggested. "I hear you can get married now at a drive-up window. Chapel Bell. The ceremony comes with a dozen tacos and a quart of guacamole."

Clair rolled her eyes, but laughed. "I just might consider that. Especially since the church in Wolf River is booked with weddings for the next few weeks. We considered an outdoor service, but with the unpredictable weather, we decided to have the ceremony in one of the ballrooms."

"Chapel Bell, I'm telling you." Evan looked at Marcy. "What do you think?"

"I think it's an interesting idea," Marcy muttered.

"Don't encourage the man." Clair furrowed her forehead when she saw the thoughtful expression on Marcy's face. "You aren't serious, are you?"

"Not the Vegas part," Marcy said with a dismissive wave of her hand. "The chapel part."

Marcy could never explain how ideas came to her, they just did. She'd learned over the years not to squelch them, but to give them free rein and see where they took her. Sometimes an idea, even one that started off as the most ridiculous thought imaginable, could turn into something amazing.

"You could build one right here," Marcy said. "This patio is beautiful, but between the heat and uncertain weather, it's probably not usable a good portion of the year. You could convert it into an enclosed garden chapel and have the feel of the outdoors no matter what the weather is, then offer wedding-reception services all year round."

When Clair and Evan just stared at her without saying anything, Marcy shifted awkwardly, then picked up her coffee cup. "Just a thought."

"It's a *wonderful* thought." Clair looked at Evan, a mixture of excitement and hope in her blue eyes. "Would it be possible to build something like that in three weeks?"

"It's possible." Evan glanced around the patio. "Especially with the right crew. And even if we didn't finish, it seems the worst that could happen is you go back to your original idea with the ceremony in the ballroom."

"A gazebo ceiling would be beautiful." Marcy could picture it now. Blond maple or oak and a white-iron chandelier hanging from the center. "With French doors that can be opened when the weather is nice."

Evan took in the area they had to work with. "French doors would be good around the back and side, but we should enclose the front half with drywall and build a raised platform."

She nodded. "If you use the same stone as the floor, I can create a garden area on both sides of the steps."

"I love it already!" Clair jumped up and hugged Marcy, then kissed her cheek. "You're brilliant."

"Hey, how 'bout me?" Evan stuck his cheek out. "I gave her the idea."

Clair hugged and kissed Evan, too. "Where do we start, what do we do, who should we—" The excitement drained from her face. "Wait. No. Neither one of you is here to work. I can't let you do this."

Evan looked at Marcy and grinned. She smiled back. "Just try and stop us," he said.

"Oh, I love you both!" There were tears in Clair's eyes. "I can't wait to tell Jacob."

"Tell me what?"

Marcy glanced up and saw the man standing in the doorway. There was no mistaking the Carver family resemblance, she thought. Same dark hair and devastating grin, same angular features. He looked a little travel weary, stubbled beard and rumpled white shirt, but it only added to his rough-around-the-edges good looks.

"Jacob!" Clair spun, then ran to Jacob and threw herself in his arms.

When they kissed, Marcy politely looked away. Shaking his head, Evan sighed and sat back in his chair. "This could take a while. You want a warm-up on your coffee, a newspaper to read, maybe a novel?"

But Clair was already pulling Jacob across the patio. "Jacob, this is Marcy. Marcy, Jacob."

Jacob's hand closed over Marcy's. "I've heard a lot about you," he said.

Marcy smiled. "And I, you."

"Sweetheart, you won't believe this." Clair slid her arms around Jacob's waist. "Marcy and Evan are going to build a chapel for us. Right here."

Jacob lifted an eyebrow and looked at Evan. "In three weeks?"

Evan nodded. "We'll need to get some plans and a crew together right away, but that shouldn't take more than a couple of days. We can probably pop this puppy out in two weeks." Evan grinned at his brother. "I might even put a hammer in your soft hands."

"We'll see who's soft," Jacob said with good nature. "Last time I saw you on the site, all you did was stand around and look pretty while you barked orders at everyone else."

"Now can I help it if I'm pretty?" Evan said with a shrug, then looked at Marcy. "He always was jealous 'cause I got the looks."

"Enough of the brotherly love," Clair said, shaking her

head. "Marcy, Evan, you have carte blanche on this. Whatever you want, whatever it costs, you got it." Clair looked
up at Jacob. "Now we have to go make that ugly mug of
yours presentable so we can have our pictures taken."

Jacob frowned, then shook his head and kissed Clair.
"There isn't another woman on this earth I'd do this
for," he said against her lips.

"I love you, too," Clair said with a smile and kissed
him again. "Maybe we can be a few minutes late."

"You know it, darlin'."

Arm in arm, Clair and Jacob walked back into the
hotel. Marcy sighed, then looked at Evan, who was still
shaking his head at the lovebirds' retreat.

The enormity of the project ahead of them suddenly
sucked the breath out of her. "We can do this, right?"

"No sweat. We'll probably need a lot of this, though,"
he said, picking up his coffee. "And we'll have to work
closely together."

Her pulse skipped at the thought. "It's for a good
cause."

"We'll have to put in a lot of hours to get the plans
drawn up this quickly and coordinate all the work."

"That's fine."

He leaned in closer. "We'll probably have to work
some nights, too."

Her pulse went from skipping to an all-out sprint.
"Whatever it takes."

His gaze dropped to her mouth and Marcy held her
breath. When he glanced up quickly and looked behind
her, she started to turn, but he caught her chin in his hand.

"Don't turn around," he said, lowering his voice. "Someone's looking this way."

"Who?"

"Take off your glasses," he whispered.

Quickly, she slipped them off. "Are they still looking?"

"Yeah. Uh-oh. They're coming this way. Better make this good."

"Make what—"

He answered her question by dropping his mouth on hers.

Four

Dear Marcy,
I've invited my boyfriend's mother and father to dinner and I want my table to look special without spending a lot of money on fancy china or silverware. What do you suggest?
Melissa in Queens

Like the first time Evan had kissed her, Marcy was too stunned to move. Too stunned to breathe.

But this time—unlike the first time—she kissed him back.

She couldn't imagine who was more surprised, herself, or Evan. But when his lips touched hers, she knew she didn't want to pull away. She'd spent half the night fantasizing about this man. How could she let this opportunity pass, even if it wasn't for real?

She couldn't.

Not that she wasn't nervous, of course. Heavens, her

heart was slamming in her chest, and her lungs refused
to draw in air. But he'd told her to make it look good,
hadn't he? Even if kissing wasn't in her area of exper-
tise, she could certainly give it her best effort. Whenever she'd put her mind to a project, she always gave it
one hundred and ten per cent.

She leaned into Evan and laid her palms flat on his
chest. His lips were firm against hers; he tasted like cin-
namon and apple. The scent of his aftershave made her
think of thick, dark woods and damp, mossy earth. Sensations rippled through her like satin ribbons of brilliant
color.

Incredible.

She felt his hesitation when she moved her mouth
against his, the momentary flex of his strong muscles
under the palms of her hands. She was certain he was
going to pull away from her, that Evan's idea of making something look good and hers were two entirely different things. Disappointment and embarrassment
flooded through her.

But he didn't pull away. Instead, he slid his hand behind her neck and tugged her closer, slanted his mouth
against hers, then slowly traced her bottom lip with his
tongue.

Amazing.

There were more sensations now. Unfamiliar, yet
exciting. Thrilling. Tiny, intense arrows of pleasure
shooting through her. Even if someone was watching
her and Evan, at this moment, she simply didn't care.

The only thing that mattered in the whole world was the feel of his mouth on hers and the hot, moist slide of his tongue over her lips.

When he slipped inside, she shivered.

Her curiosity became a startling desire, and she curled her fingers into the soft cotton of his T-shirt. She could feel the heat of his body under her hands, the steady thud of his heart. Her own heart was racing. Her skin felt tight, her breasts ached. With every stroke of his tongue, a need she'd never experienced before intensified. It frightened and thrilled her at the same time.

She wasn't sure if it was the sound of a distant lawnmower or the chirping of a bird from a nearby tree, but a noise invaded her muddled brain, bringing reason back.

Blinking her eyes open, she pulled away, then reached for her glasses and slid them back on. Prayed her hands weren't shaking too badly. She couldn't look at him, was afraid if she did, she would see what had just happened didn't mean anything to him, or worse, that he might even find amusement in her inexperience.

"Are they gone?" she asked, struggling to control her emotions.

"Yeah." His voice had a rough edge to it. "You're safe."

Safe? Good Lord, she was anything but "safe" around this man!

"So," he said quietly, "shall we go to my room, or yours?"

Shocked, Marcy looked up, was relieved to see there

was no amusement in his eyes or indifference, either. Anything but. His dark brown gaze held more than a glint of desire.

My room or yours?

She swallowed hard. No man had ever asked her *that* before.

Still, the best she could manage was a mouselike squeak. "What?"

"I've got drafting supplies in my room," he said. "We'll need to sketch some rough plans and have Clair look them over, then I can get exact measurements later and use a computer to draw the blueprints."

"Oh, right." Of course he hadn't been suggesting anything more than work. She felt as ridiculous over her assumption as she did at her disappointment. "Your room is fine."

At least work was one area of her life where she felt completely confident and comfortable. *I'm a professional,* she told herself. As long as she stayed focused on the project, she wouldn't be thinking about Evan in a physical manner.

But even as she followed him to the elevators, even as she turned her mind to the task at hand, her lips still tingled and her skin still burned and she knew the next three weeks were indeed going to be a challenge.

Watching Marcy work was almost as incredible as kissing her, Evan decided two hours later. One minute she was doodling on a pad of paper, the next she was talking to herself.

At the moment, she was doing both while she paced back and forth from the living- to dining-room area.

She hardly seemed to know he was in the room, though every so often she'd look at him, glasses on top of her head, and her eyes would widen with some new idea. Then she'd quickly jot down a note with the pencil she'd stuck behind her ear.

He sat at the dining-room table, scratching out basic designs one after the other, an exploration of different ideas, each sketch building on the one before. He knew they were getting closer to the final design and were down to details now.

He respected the fact that she was a perfectionist, had been accused of the same crime himself. In the building trade, Evan had met far too many people who settled for "good enough," but he had no tolerance for sloppy work or cutting corners. It had taken him years to find the right crew and suppliers, men and women who were as meticulous as he was. Some of them were pain-in-the-butt prima donnas, but he tolerated their idiosyncrasies, just as they tolerated his.

He slid the sketch he'd been working on—his tenth—across the table. "How's this?"

"Almost." Tapping her chin, she studied the drawing. "I think the ceiling should be a little higher for a more cathedral look. A wedding is a spiritual and emotional joining of two people. A promise of forever. The environment we create has to support and give credence to that promise. Not just with our minds, or hearts, but with our souls."

He didn't know what to say to that. Hearts and promises and forever weren't exactly his forte. But he knew she wasn't really looking for an answer, anyway. In the past two hours, he'd learned that was how she operated. She'd ask herself a question or make a comment, roll it around in her brain, pull it apart, then put it back together until all the pieces fit neatly into place.

He'd also learned she really didn't need her glasses except for fine print, she didn't like ice in her water, and she'd never seen a reality show. He felt as if he already knew more about Marcy than most of the women he'd dated.

He watched her pluck a pencil from behind her ear, then sketch a rectangular window on the drawing and slide it back. "How about a stained-glass window right here? The light streaming through will give the room an ethereal look."

He nodded. "Good idea, but we won't have time to have it built, so that gives us two weeks at the most to find one premade."

Marcy's face lit with enthusiasm. "The thrill of the hunt gets the blood pumping, my Aunt Hattie used to say just before we'd go to the local flea market every Saturday."

He thought if she kept looking at him like that, with her cheeks flushed and her green eyes glittering, she was going to get *his* blood pumping right here and now.

He'd kissed her earlier on an impulse, an irresistible urge to wipe that prim look from her face. He'd also figured that if they were going to be working together, he should just get it out of the way, rather than wasting time wondering. He'd intended it to be a simple, friendly kiss.

Then she'd gone and done the unexpected.

She'd kissed him back.

And there'd been nothing simple about it at all. Nothing friendly. It had been *hot*. Arousing.

Disturbing.

He didn't like being off balance like that. He prided himself on control, especially when it came to women and sex. But when she'd pressed those soft, warm lips of hers against his, when she'd laid her hands on his chest and made that small sound in her throat, he'd lost it. All he could think was that he wanted to drag her upstairs, take her to his bed and finish what he'd started.

"Oh, Evan, I think that's a wonderful idea."

Startled, he looked up at her. Good God, could she read minds, too, or had he said out loud what he'd been thinking? "What's a wonderful idea?"

"The arch in the doorway here. I love that." She stood behind him, looking over his shoulder at his sketch. "We could even paint climbing roses and give it the feeling of an arbor."

He'd been so preoccupied thinking about making love to Marcy, he'd barely realized what he'd drawn.

She leaned in and tapped her fingertip to his drawing. "Right here we could arch the area over the French doors and the stained-glass window, too. It will give the room a softer effect."

Evan was used to working closely with his clients in the design stage, but he'd never worked quite this close, or been quite so distracted before. Marcy's scent reminded him of the honeysuckle that had grown wild behind the apartment house he'd lived in when he was a kid. He remembered how sweet the flower tasted if you pulled it off the vine and sucked on it.

That thought stimulated more than a memory.

"Oh, and right here—" oblivious to his discomfort, she reached in closer, absently brushing her arm against his "—this is where the bride will enter, so I think a higher, wider doorway will have a more dramatic impact."

She paused for a moment, deep in thought, and then she was off again, pacing and making notes.

He let out the breath he'd been holding. Good God. He could barely keep up with her. And though he told himself not to, he couldn't help but wonder what all that excess energy of hers would be like in bed.

It was an interesting thought.

He didn't intend to sleep with her, of course. Kissing her was one thing. Taking her to bed was another matter entirely. It would be awkward, at best. Not only because she was Clair's friend, but somehow, he didn't really think Marcy was the let's-have-a-wild-night-of-sex-then-go-our-own-way kind of girl.

She was more the let's-pick-out-rings type.

He shuddered at the thought, then turned his attention back to the sketch he was drawing, adding in the doorway and window she'd suggested and realized she'd been right. She truly had an amazing eye for design and detail. He glanced up at her, watched her touch the pencil to her lips, lightly stroking it back and forth.

Dammit.

If this was any other woman, he might have thought she was intentionally teasing him. But this was Marcy, and he was certain she didn't have a clue that she was driving him crazy.

When she started to nibble on the eraser, his hand tightened and he snapped the lead on his pencil.

"Marcy."

"Hmm?"

"Stop that."

"Stop what?"

"Chewing on your pencil."

She furrowed her forehead. "That bothers you?"

"As a matter of fact, it does," he said. When she looked at him, confused, he frowned. "It's bad for your teeth."

"It is?" She slid her glasses from the top of her head back onto her nose and stared at the pencil.

"Yeah." Well, it *could* be, he thought, then rolled his shoulders and leaned back in his chair. "Why don't we take a break?"

"Okay. I'll go to my room and you can—"

"Sit."

"No, really, I should—"

"Sit." Using his foot, he pushed one of the chairs away from the table.

She hesitated, then sat down, but her back was stiff as a two-by-four and he figured if he put a level to her shoulders, she'd be plumb. Unbidden, the thought came to him and he smiled.

Sugarplumb.

"Tell me about this aunt of yours," he said.

"Aunt Hattie?" Marcy tucked her hair behind her ears. "Well, she was my mother's sister, twelve years her senior. We lived in the same town. After my parents died, she took me in."

He watched her pick up a scrap of paper from the table and fiddle with it. "How did they die?"

"We had an old house, faulty wiring," Marcy said quietly. "My parents' bedroom was in the back of the house and the firemen couldn't reach them in time. All I remember is waking up on my front lawn and my aunt was holding me, crying. I was only eight."

Evan resisted the urge to cover her hands and still those busy fingers of hers. "That's a tough one." Hell, what else was there to say? he thought.

"Everyone used to call Henrietta Thatcher eccentric. She made sculptures out of old iron and odds and ends she found in the junkyard or on the side of the road." Marcy smiled. "Now that I've made a name for myself, they call her a character. She sells her work in galleries across the country."

Marcy set the piece of paper she'd been folding on the palm of her hand. She'd made a tiny bird, Evan realized. Lifting an eyebrow, he looked at her.

"It works with napkins, too," she said. "If you're having a dinner party, it spruces up a table. I'd be happy to teach you."

He could just see himself folding napkins for a dinner party in his trailer—or anywhere, for that matter. That would happen the same day he took up knitting and candle making.

"I'll let you know," he said with a chuckle, then set the bird on the table and took her hands in his. "Marcy, I think we should talk about what happened this morning on the patio."

Her gaze dropped. "You're right, we should. I apologize."

He frowned at her. "What?"

"Well, I know you were just trying to prevent someone from recognizing me, and I, well, I got a little carried away in the moment."

"Marcy—"

"You're a very good kisser," she said in a matter-of-fact tone. "But I'm sure you know that already."

"Marcy—"

"I didn't mean to put you in an awkward situation," she went on. "Especially since we're working together. But I assure you, I won't do that again and if you want, I—"

"Marcy!" In one swift move, he leaned forward and dropped his mouth over hers, a quick kiss, then he sat back down.

Eyes wide, she looked at him.

"Marcy," he said firmly. "I didn't kiss you this morning because anyone was looking at you. I kissed you because I wanted to."

"Because you wanted to?" Her eyes grew wider still. "Why?"

"It's called spontaneity. I felt like kissing you, so I did. Is that so hard to understand?"

"Well," she said, shifting awkwardly. "Actually, it is."

"And why is that?"

"Let's just say I'm not the type who normally motivates spontaneity."

Before he'd met her—certainly before he'd kissed her—he probably would have agreed with her. But definitely not now.

"It's not that I don't appreciate it," she went on when he didn't say anything. "And I certainly enjoyed it. But it's just that, well, I think it's best if it doesn't happen again."

That, he agreed with, but still, he'd like to hear Marcy's reasoning on the subject. "Why is that?"

"Number one, we're going to be working together and it's distracting."

True. It was damn distracting.

"Number two, it can't go anywhere, so it would just be—" she blushed "—frustrating."

Very true, but he couldn't resist asking her, "Where exactly were you thinking 'it' can't go?"

Her blush deepened. "The natural development of a mutual attraction would probably lead to the next step of intimacy."

He couldn't help but grin at her. "Gosh, I like it when a woman talks dirty. I can hardly wait to hear number three."

"Number three," she said softly and raised her gaze to meet his, "is that I like you."

I like you? He lifted an eyebrow. Well now, this was a first. A woman didn't want to be "intimate" with him because she liked him.

"You're going to be my best friend's brother-in-law," she said. "I'm certain that we'll see each other from time to time. If we were to—if we—"

"Slept together?"

Nodding, she lowered her gaze. "I'm sure you'll agree it would be awkward."

He leaned back in his chair. A woman's logic, he thought with a sigh. He knew better than to argue with that.

And besides, she was right, dammit.

"Fine. I won't kiss you again. We'll just concentrate on getting this chapel built. How's that?"

"Great," she said with such a bright, sunny smile that he didn't know whether to be insulted or pleased.

When the phone rang, Evan moved into the living area to answer it, grateful for a reason to not only stretch his legs, but put some distance between himself and Marcy. "May I speak with Marcy Pruitt, please?" a woman said on the other end of the line.

"Marcy Pruitt?"

Marcy's gaze snapped up.

"Tell her it's Anna."

"Anna who?"

Marcy was up on her feet and had the phone out of his hands. "What's wrong?"

He watched Marcy's face turn pale as she listened. Whoever Anna was, and whatever she had to say, didn't appear to be good news.

"Are you sure about this?" Marcy dragged a hand through her hair. "All right. I promise I won't say anything. Call me in the morning, but don't use the office phone."

"Problem?" he asked when she hung up the phone.

"I'm going to kill Helen."

"Your manager?"

"My *ex*-manager," she said tightly. "I can't believe she would do this. Even for Helen, this is extreme."

"What did she do?"

Marcy pressed her lips into a thin line. "She hired a private investigator to find me."

Five

Dear Marcy,
I am in charge of planning my friends' wedding
shower. Do you have any suggestions for games
at a shower that can include men and women?
Arlene from Indianapolis

"She hired a private investigator?"

Marcy stared blankly at the phone. "Anna said she overheard Helen talking on her cell phone. She only caught bits and pieces of the conversation, but from what she could gather, Helen has actually hired someone to find me."

"Whoa." Evan whistled softly. "Isn't that a little extreme?"

"That's Helen's middle name." As the reality of it seeped into her brain, so did the anger. "I'm going to kill her."

"Why don't you just fire her?" Evan asked.

"There'd be no pleasure in that." Hands fisted, Marcy started to pace. "I can't believe this."

"So you're saying you're *not* going to fire her?"

Marcy reached the sofa, then spun on her heels and headed back toward the dining-room table. "I can't do that."

"Surely any contract you have won't hold up under something like this."

Marcy marched back toward the sofa again, shaking her head. "We don't have a contract."

"You're kidding me." He stared at her in disbelief. "How is that possible?"

"I know how incredible that sounds, but we've never needed one. I trust Helen completely."

"What a minute." Frowning, Evan snagged her arm before she could get away again. "You're making me dizzy. Sit."

When she sank down on the chair beside him, he put his hands on both sides of her knees and leaned in. "Are we talking about the same woman here? The one who just hired a P.I. to find you?"

"Our relationship isn't based on lawyers and contracts and legalities," Marcy said. "As foolish as it might seem to you, it's based on faith and friendship. Helen might be controlling and demanding, but she would never do anything to hurt me."

"This doesn't hurt you?"

"No." She pressed her lips firmly together. "But it does make me mad."

He shook his head. "I don't get it."

She tried not to focus on the fact that Evan had moved into her space, or the fact that his hands were a fraction away from touching her legs. And she desperately tried not to think about the fact that he had kissed her—for the second time that day—only a few moments ago.

"You have to understand our history," she said with a sigh. "After college I moved to Los Angeles and started my own catering company. I had steady bookings, but the competition was fierce and I didn't know how to run the financial aspect of a business. After a year I had an Everest-size mountain of bills and was two months late on my rent. I was broke and tired and ready to give up. And then I met Helen."

Marcy remembered how lonely she'd been, living in a tiny apartment in West L.A., working out of an even smaller office and kitchen. "I was catering a birthday party for a Hollywood producer. I thought it would be my last job and I would make just enough to pay my bills and maybe gas to get back to Burbridge. Helen approached me at the party, told me that I made the best chocolate soufflé she'd ever had. She also said I had something, a look, a style, that she could market. She gave me her card and told me that within three years Marcy Pruitt was going to be a household name. I laughed at her, of course, and thought she was a nutcase. I didn't even call her back. But she showed up at my apartment as I was packing my bags, then took me to lunch and laid out her plan. Three hours later, she put me up in a hotel, had six celebrity parties booked for me, and was already working on the layout for my first how-to book."

"That's admirable," Evan said evenly, "but, honey, she made a lot of money on you."

"She earned every penny and still does." No one worked harder or with more dedication than Helen, Marcy thought. "What really mattered was that she believed in me, even when I didn't believe in myself. She never gave up or let up. Everything I have, where I am today, I owe it all to her."

"I can understand you're grateful," Evan said, shaking his head. "What I don't understand is what she hopes to accomplish by hiring a P.I. to track you down, unless she plans on having you tied up and dragged back to Los Angeles."

"If she could get away with it, she might." Marcy smiled at the thought. "But really I think she just wants to know where I am and that I'm all right. On top of being tenacious, she's also a worrier."

"So why don't you just call her up and let her know you're on to her, then tell her to back off?"

"If I'm ever going to have any time to myself, I need Helen to learn to trust Anna to make decisions. If Helen finds out that Anna told me about the P.I., I'm afraid she might not work with her at all. And then I'll *have* to go back."

"Women." Evan sighed, then took Marcy's hand in his and balled her fingers into a fist. "Guys could just duke it out and move on."

When Evan's hand closed over hers, Marcy's heart stuttered. "I'd rather you didn't mention this to Clair just yet. She's got a lot on her mind right now. She doesn't need to worry about me, too."

"She needs to know, Marcy. She can alert her staff and beef up her security here."

"I'll tell her after the party tonight," Marcy said, then pulled her hand from Evan's. "We should get back to work if we're going to finish the final sketch today. Clair and Jacob will be back anytime now, and you've got a fitting this afternoon."

"Fittings and showers." He rolled his head back and groaned. "Las Vegas, I'm telling you. The only way to go."

Lucas and Julianna Blackhawk lived in a two-story blue-gray clapboard a few miles outside of town. Not an especially large house, Evan thought as he pulled into the gravel-lined circular driveway, but it definitely had appeal. White shutters, front porch, beds of blooming roses and colorful flowers. To the west of the house, a stand of trees lined a creek bed. To the east, horses grazed inside a white-fenced pasture. The surrounding land, thousands of acres of Blackhawk ranch, stretched as far as the eye could see.

There were several cars already parked in front of the house and Evan pulled his truck alongside a black SUV, then shut off the engine. "Here we are."

When Marcy didn't respond, he glanced across the seat at her. Deep in thought, she stared out the car window, fiddling with the pearl necklace she wore. The black sheath she had on wasn't exactly sexy, he thought, but it suited her conservative style. Her shoes, also black, had a low heel, nothing intended to stir a man's blood.

And yet, nonetheless, his blood did stir. There was something about this woman. He wasn't sure what it was. Just…something. He wondered if that's what Helen had seen in Marcy—that undefinable "it" that so many celebrities had. Helen had obviously recognized Marcy's universal appeal and packaged it.

The manager might be a female snake, but she was one smart snake.

He came around and opened Marcy's door, then surprised her by wrapping his hands around her waist and lifting her out of the truck.

"Evan!" She laid a hand on his chest to steady herself. "That wasn't necessary."

"It's a long step down." He let his hands linger on her waist even after he set her on the ground. "You look pretty tonight."

"Thank you." She blushed at his compliment. "And you look handsome."

"Thanks." Reluctantly, he let go of her, then tugged at the tie choking him. He'd drawn the line on a suit, but had compromised with a sport coat and slacks. By the time this wedding business was over, he figured his brother was going to owe him big-time.

"After you."

He followed behind her, appreciating the sway of her hips as she moved up the front steps. The scent of Italian spices drifted on the warm, early-evening air, mixing with the sound of animated conversations from inside the house.

"By the way," he said, leaning in close as he knocked on the front door, "you've got great legs."

She looked at him, eyes wide, but didn't have time to respond before Lucas opened the door.

Smiling, he followed her inside. This party just might be fun, after all, he decided.

Marcy decided that walking into Lucas and Julianna's home was a bit like white-water rafting. From the moment Lucas had opened the door with his six-month-old son in his arms, there had been an endless, swiftly moving current of introductions, enthusiastic handshakes and unexpected warm hugs. The Blackhawks were a bit overwhelming, a little wild and definitely noisy.

Marcy liked them immediately.

While she sipped a glass of wine and waited for the guests of honor to arrive, Marcy stepped back from the hubbub and mentally ran through the introductions again.

Rand and Seth, Clair's brothers, were easy to remember. They had Clair's smile and thick, shiny dark hair. Rand's wife, Grace, a lovely redhead, was perhaps the most elegant woman at the party, while Hannah, Seth's wife, had a homespun beauty with dazzling blue eyes and a mop of blond curls. And though Marcy still wasn't sure who belonged to whom, it seemed to her that there were children everywhere. She watched at least a half-dozen youngsters, screaming and giggling, race down the stairs and fly out the front door, while the adults, seemingly oblivious to the ruckus, never missed a beat in their conversations.

There were two other couples at the party Marcy had met, friends that Clair had made since moving to Wolf River. Nick Santos and his wife, Maggie, who were expecting their third child and Clay and Paige Bodine, who were expecting their second.

"I've decided it's something in the water."

Marcy turned. A beautiful woman with shoulder-length auburn hair stood next to her.

"Olivia Cameron."

She held out her hand and Marcy took it, couldn't help but notice the exquisite silver rings and bracelets she wore. "Marcy Pruitt. What's in the water?"

"The wedding-and-baby bug." Olivia looked across the room while she sipped from her wineglass. "At least I hope it's the water. If it's airborne, we're all doomed."

Marcy smiled. "You're the antique dealer and interior designer Clair told me about. I love what you did with the lobby at the hotel."

"Thanks." Pleasure sparkled in Olivia's soft blue eyes. "But I saw the 'Marcy's Makeover' article your magazine did on that turn-of-the-century farmhouse. It was amazing. I'm still drooling over the antiques you pulled out of the basement."

That project had been one of Marcy's favorites. Tourists had bypassed the bed-and-breakfast in northern California's wine country for years and the owners had sent in a plea for help. Since the article, Marcy had heard that business was booming.

"There were some great antiques in the barn you might be interested in," Marcy said. "I can call the owner for you. Oh, and I'd like to come by and see your store, too. If you wouldn't mind, I'd like to include you in a feature we'll be doing on small-town antique stores."

"If I wouldn't mind?" Olivia stared at Marcy. "You're kidding, right?"

"Not at all. I could interview you before I go back to L.A., then after the wedding, I can send a photographer."

"Well, I—" Olivia put a hand to her throat and made a choking sound. "Sure."

"You okay?" Frowning, Julianna came over with a tray of tiny crab cakes. "Can I get you some water?"

When Marcy and Olivia looked at each other and laughed, Julianna furrowed her forehead.

"Olivia thinks all the weddings and babies have something to do with the water," Marcy explained.

"Is that what it is?" Julianna smiled, then looked at her husband, who was tossing their newest child into the air and making the baby laugh hysterically. "I'll have to make sure I drink my eight glasses a day, then."

"She's lost." Olivia rolled her eyes. "But do tell. Who is that gorgeous man standing next to Lucas, and please tell me he's not married or engaged."

When Marcy turned to see who Olivia was referring to, her stomach twisted in a knot.

"That's Evan, Jacob's brother. Would you like to meet him?"

Olivia arched an eyebrow. "Oh, yeah."

"I have to go check on my lasagna first," Julianna said, "then I'll take you over."

"I can introduce you," Marcy said politely.

Olivia frowned, then her eyes widened. "Ohmigod. Are you here with him? I'm so sorry, I didn't—"

"No." Marcy shook her head. "He just drove me here from the hotel, that's all. I'm not here with him. I barely know him."

"Are you sure? Because if there's something—"

"There isn't." Marcy smiled her TV smile. "Really, I'd be happy to introduce you."

"That's not necessary." Olivia locked her gaze on Evan and sipped her wine. "I think I can find my way over there."

"Watch out, boys." Julianna smiled when Olivia walked away. "Here she comes."

"Evan can manage," Marcy said thoughtfully.

"If he's anything like Jacob, I imagine he can," Julianna said with a nod. "Excuse me one minute, will you?"

"Can I help you in the kitchen?" Marcy offered, wanting something, anything, to keep her busy.

"Thank you, but absolutely not. You're here to relax, not work." The children ran in the back door and up the stairs, all of them screaming like banshees. Julianna looked at Marcy, then sighed and walked off, mumbling, "Maybe I should stick to bottled water from now on."

Marcy glanced at Evan, watched him smile at Olivia, then shake her hand. The woman was beautiful, single and obviously not interested in marriage or children. They'd make a perfect match.

The knot in her stomach tightened.

Not quite ready to join back in the party, she wandered outside onto a raised, covered patio. The sun was dipping low on the horizon and though it was still warm, the air had cooled several degrees. Beyond the wide expanse of freshly mowed grass and children's lawn toys were two corrals and a tall, red barn. To the left of the house, on the far edge of the lawn, she could hear a creek running below a white gazebo.

She turned at the sound of laughter from inside the house. The Blackhawks were certainly a lively bunch. Animated conversations, genuine laughter, sincerity in their obvious affection for each other. She'd missed that growing up—family gatherings on holidays, weddings to celebrate, babies to coo over.

It didn't take a rocket scientist to figure out why she'd started her career in catering. Planning parties gave her the connection with people she'd so badly needed. She'd always taken great pleasure watching people enjoy themselves, had never minded standing on the sidelines. Her work had been her greatest joy and she'd thrown herself into it.

She turned and rested her arms on the patio railing, glanced at the children's toys on the lawn, the redwood boxes of tomatoes and squash, the carefully tended beds of flowers. And suddenly she knew all that she had, all that she'd accomplished, wasn't enough anymore. She wanted this in her life, too. This bond of family, the connection of friends. And a home. Not just a house—she had a house—but a *home*.

She knew it was her attraction to Evan that had stoked the home fires in her. She'd never felt anything like this before. This breath-stealing, heart-pounding, flutter-in-the-stomach feeling. It was new and exciting, and while she knew that a relationship with Evan was out of the question, he'd definitely opened her eyes to the possibilities.

By the way, you've got great legs.

Remembering what he'd whispered to her just before Lucas had opened the door made her smile. He'd done that on purpose, she thought. Tried to throw her off-kilter. She supposed he couldn't help himself, saying and doing outrageous things like that. She certainly knew she couldn't take him seriously.

But she'd be lying to herself if she didn't admit that his compliment had felt good.

It had felt great.

"Hiding out?"

Surprised at the sound of Evan's voice, Marcy

glanced over her shoulder, was even more surprised that Olivia wasn't with him.

"Just enjoying the view," she said honestly.

A bottle of beer in his hand, he moved across the patio toward her. He'd already loosened his tie, and the casual gesture only increased his rugged appeal.

"Don't you have views in Los Angeles?" he asked, leaning on the rail beside her.

"Not like this." She watched a horse stroll across one of the corrals. "Have you ever been there?"

"Never had a reason to." He reached out and tucked a loose strand of hair behind her ear. "But you'll be the first to know if I do."

The brush of his fingertips on her ear sent a jolt through her. She stiffened at the contact, watched him lift his beer bottle and tip his head back to drink. Her own throat went dry.

"Marcy Pruitt, when did you plan on telling me what's going on?"

Marcy jumped back at the sound of Clair's voice. When she turned, Clair was standing at the patio door, frowning. Jacob was right behind her, looking very guilty.

Flustered, Marcy stepped away from Evan. "Nothing's going on."

"I know you had an urgent phone call this afternoon from Los Angeles that was forwarded to Evan's room," Clair said. "It seems that everyone, including my future husband, knows what that phone call was about but me." Clair turned her frown on Jacob. "And he's not talking."

Oh, thank goodness. Clair was referring to the private investigator. Marcy breathed a silent sigh of relief. And she'd thought that Clair—well, it didn't matter what she'd thought.

Marcy narrowed her eyes and looked at Evan. "You weren't supposed to say anything."

"Well, actually," he scratched the back of his neck, "you asked me not to say anything to Clair. But I thought Jacob should look into it."

"Look into what?" Clair threw her hands out in exasperation. "Somebody tell me what's going on before I scream."

"My manager hired a private investigator to find me," Marcy said.

"What!" Clair's mouth dropped open. "This is someone who works for you?"

Marcy sighed. "To say the least, she's tenacious."

Clair made a rude sound. "Tenacity is fine in business, but honey, this is your personal life."

That was the problem, Marcy realized. She'd never had a personal life, and Helen didn't know quite what to make of it. *For that matter, I'm not quite sure myself,* she thought. But she really didn't care to admit that in front of Evan and Jacob.

"I'd like to give that woman a piece of my mind," Clair said through clenched teeth. "I'd tell her to—"

"Let's talk about this later, shall we?" Jacob took

hold of Clair's shoulders. "I called a friend of mine in L.A. He's going to ask around, see what he can find out. In the meantime, we'll keep our eyes open for anyone suspicious, either in town, or at the hotel."

Jacob slipped his arms around his bride-to-be and kissed the top of her head. Clair's shoulders relaxed, then she leaned into him, the movement as natural and unconscious as breathing. It was a beautiful thing, Marcy thought, a rare thing, to see two people this much in love.

In spite of her happiness for them both, Marcy couldn't stop the twinge of envy. Ashamed of herself, she quickly shoved the feeling out of her mind. This was not the time to be thinking about her own love life—or lack of one, anyway.

"It's not as if you both don't have enough to do, and now you have to baby-sit me, too?" Marcy shook her head. "I didn't come here to be a bother."

"Watching out for a friend is hardly baby-sitting or a bother," Jacob said. "And besides, you didn't come here to work, either, and here you are, designing a wedding chapel."

"That's not work, that's fun," she said truthfully.

"So how soon can we see what you two have done?" Clair asked, her eyes bright with excitement.

"I'll have the basic plan drawn tomorrow morning," Evan said.

"Not that she's being pushy or anything." Jacob gave Clair a squeeze. "She talked about it all afternoon, and

I had to physically restrain her from going to Evan's room and bothering you two."

"Is that what you call what you were doing?" Clair asked, lifting one eyebrow.

Grinning, Jacob planted a quick kiss on Clair's mouth.

Evan looked at Marcy and shook his head. "Nauseating, ain't it?" he said.

Marcy thought it was wonderful, but she refrained from commenting.

"We should get back inside." Clair took Jacob's hand. "Julianna says we have to play The Almost-Newlywed Game before we eat dinner. If I win, you have to write a poem for me and recite it in front of everyone."

"Like hell," Jacob said with a snort, then thought for a moment. "So what happens if *I* win?"

"I have to model all the lingerie I get at the shower for you. In private, of course."

"Is that so?" Grinning, he wiggled his eyebrows, then took Clair's hand. "Well, then, let the games begin."

Evan shook his head after Clair and Jacob went back in the house. "Six months ago, if anyone had told me that my brother would be willingly playing a game at his own wedding shower and agreeing to write a poem, I would have said they were drunk or just plain crazy."

"Love can do that," Marcy said softly, staring after the moonstruck couple.

He moved beside her, then leaned against the porch rail and grinned at her. "Make you act stupid?"

She studied him over the rim of her glass. Underneath the teasing smile, she could see he was dead serious. "Apparently, you've never been in love."

"I like to keep my sanity, thank you very much."

There was a certain amount of reason in that, she supposed. "It's exhilarating. Wonderfully, horribly thrilling, and you just know you'll die if that person doesn't love you back."

"Gosh, that sounds like fun." He looked as if he'd just sniffed something that had been forgotten in the back of a refrigerator. "So what was the lucky guy's name?"

"Leo Fitzmeyer."

He arched one eyebrow. "Leo Fitzmeyer?"

"He had the most amazing eyes." Smiling at the memory, she sipped her wine. "Every girl in the fifth grade was madly in love with him."

"Ah." His grin widened. "Lucky Leo."

He moved in closer and Marcy's nerves began jangling like a fire bell. What had she been thinking? Initiating a conversation as to whether he'd ever been in love? Talk about stupid.

"So where is Leo now?" Evan asked.

"In New York." Casually, she inched away. "He bought a hair salon in Manhattan. Very chic."

"Ah." He nodded. "I see."

"Leo has a beautiful wife and three handsome boys, all of them very definitely his." Marcy cocked her head and met Evan's gaze. "Last I heard they were trying for a girl."

"That's the fun part of kids." His grin widened. "Trying."

In spite of her determination to resist his charm, she laughed. "You don't like children?"

"Sure I do. I can't wait for Jacob and Clair to have a bunch of little rugrats. I figure I'll come visit, get them riled up, then I'll leave."

"You really are impossible," she said, shaking her head. But when she turned to leave, he took hold of her arm.

"Hey." He met her gaze, then his tone turned somber. "I just want you to know I'll be watching your back."

"I—" She hesitated, wasn't sure what to say. "Thank you."

His hand lingered for a moment, then dropped away at the sudden burst of laughter from inside the house. Apparently, the game had begun. With a resigned sigh, he gestured toward the doorway. "After you, Miss Pruitt."

Six

Dear Marcy,
I've been living with the same dull, drab walls and carpet in my house for almost twenty years! I'm way past ready for a change. Can you give me a few simple tips to help me "spice up" my life?
Tina in Tulsa

It felt good to swing a hammer again. Working alongside his crew, surrounded by the buzz of saws and the smell of fresh-cut wood, all that gave Evan a sense of satisfaction no office job ever could. At least at the end of the day, he thought, he could take a step back and see what he'd accomplished.

Slipping his hammer into the work belt around his hips, he wiped at the sweat on his forehead and took a step back now. They'd managed to get a rush on the permits, then torn down the old patio cover, poured the foundation and were moving swiftly along on the framing and electrical.

Not bad for a week's work.

He glanced overhead, watched a crane lower one of the ceiling beams onto a brace. Jacob and the site foreman, Tom, were perched on a scaffolding, helping guide a twelve-by-twelve beam into place. Everyone had worked hard in the sweltering heat these past few days, but the extra hours had paid off. They were already ahead of schedule—a rare occurrence in the construction trade.

But his men and Jacob weren't the only ones who had worked hard.

He looked at Marcy, who stood several yards away, absently running one hand over the strap of her overalls while she studied the paint samples she'd taped to a bare stud. She had a habit of losing herself in her work, becoming so completely focused that she was oblivious to the sounds and activity surrounding her.

A little *too* oblivious, he thought, scanning the area for anyone who didn't belong there.

She might not be concerned that her manager had hired a P.I. to find her, Evan thought, but he sure as hell was. Until Jacob's contact in Los Angeles could verify Anna's information and come up with a name or a face, Evan had decided they couldn't be too careful. He'd cordoned off the construction site from any curious hotel guests and made sure she'd stayed close by him all week.

His men had grumbled at first that she was in their way, always asking questions or making suggestions, but it seemed they'd not only gotten used to her being around, they'd even presented her with a hard hat and tool belt of her own. Obviously, she'd been accepted as part of the team.

Some of them had accepted her just a little *too* much, Evan thought as he watched James, one of the younger apprentices, stroll in Marcy's direction with a can of cold soda. The kid all but fell over his own feet as he offered the drink to Marcy. When she smiled and accepted the can, James actually blushed and shoved his hands into his jeans' pockets.

When James happened to glance over, Evan scowled at him. Wisely, the apprentice beat a quick retreat.

It had become apparent in the past couple of days that the kid had developed a crush on Marcy. He'd followed her around like a lovesick puppy until Evan had barked at him yesterday to get his butt back to work. The other guys had teased the apprentice, but he was an easygoing kid who took the ribbing in stride.

Personally, Evan did not see the humor in it.

Evan had spent a lot of time with Marcy this past week, not only on the job site, but in the evenings, too. Every night after the crew went home, she would come up to his room and they'd order dinner, then go over what had been accomplished to date—what would happen the next day, what had been ordered, when deliveries of materials and samples would be made. She'd stayed involved with every step of the construction, and he had to admit, her contributions of ideas and suggestions for changes as they went along had been impressive.

It was easy to see why she'd been so successful in her career. Her enthusiasm infected and inspired everyone around her. She seemed to take delight in every stud nailed into place, every wall that took shape, every window and door that was framed. It should have annoyed him that she was endlessly curious and seemed to be underfoot, but strangely, he hadn't minded. In fact, they'd worked very well together.

Made him wonder how well they might do other things together, too.

She could spout off speeches about just wanting to be friends and she *liked* him, but underneath all that rationalizing, he knew damn well she was doing some wondering herself. He also knew that whenever he moved in too close, or when his hand brushed hers, she wasn't thinking "friend." He could see it in her eyes, could feel the tension between them.

He made her nervous, and that, he decided, was a good thing.

He'd managed to keep his hands off her and maintain a professional distance, but every night when she came to his room, all he could think about was kissing her. And every night when she left, it was all he could do not to ask her to stay. Hell, they were both adults, attracted to each other, unattached. That was easy enough.

So why not?

He watched her raise the can of soda to her mouth and drink, then felt a jolt of lust when she licked her bottom lip.

Swearing, he quickly looked away, then pulled his hammer out of his belt and drove another nail into the door frame he'd been working on.

He knew why not, dammit. Because it wasn't so easy. She was different than any other woman he'd ever dated. Different from any other woman he'd ever been attracted to before. Marcy's whole life was based on hearth and home. Marriage. Kids. He wasn't ready for any of that. Didn't know if he ever would be.

She'd be going back to Los Angeles after the wedding, he'd be moving on to his next job. Marcy Pruitt wasn't the type to have a casual affair. For that matter, unless he'd completely read her wrong, she was a virgin.

A *virgin,* for crying out loud.

That alone was enough for him to keep his distance. The last thing he wanted to do was hurt her. She was delicate. Fragile. Like fine china. She deserved a hell of a lot more than he could offer her.

He drove another nail into a stud, glad that he had the type of job where he could pound some of his frustration away.

But it didn't take long before he found his attention drawn back to Marcy again, couldn't help but think she looked adorable in her hard hat, overalls and work boots. Even that silly tool belt she wore turned him on, dammit.

When James strolled back over to Marcy and started talking to her again, Evan decided he'd had enough.

He jammed his hammer back into his tool belt and stomped over. When James saw him coming, he visibly swallowed, then stumbled over an air hammer in his haste to get back to work.

Oblivious to the exchange between the two men, Marcy turned and smiled when she noticed him walking toward her.

"You're just in time to give me your opinion," she said, looking back at her paint chips.

He had an opinion, all right. She should come up to his room and get naked with him. But he doubted that was an opinion she wanted to hear.

When he noticed the EVAN CARVER CONSTRUCTION logo on the white T-shirt under her overalls, he lifted an eyebrow. "Nice T-shirt."

"Tom gave it to me. He said all the crew members have one, so I should, too. Do you mind?"

He noticed the curve of her breast directly under his logo and felt his pulse quicken. He wanted his hands and mouth there, dammit, and it irritated him that he couldn't even have a conversation with this woman and not want to touch and kiss her all over. "Why would I mind?"

She gave him an odd look, then looked back at her paint chips. "Which do you like for the French doors, Cloud Nine or Vanilla Ice?"

He wondered briefly who the hell came up with these

ridiculous names, then stepped closer and studied the samples. "Buy a quart of both. The light in here will change after the walls are up and we'll see how they look."

Nodding, she placed her hands on the small of her back and stretched. It was an innocent movement on her part, certainly not intended to evoke lust, but somehow that made her all the more appealing. Rather than take her hand and drag her upstairs, he clenched his teeth.

He *really* had to stop this line of thinking.

"Evan, this is all so wonderful," she said, glancing around the site. "I can't believe what you've managed to do in a week."

"Not me. We." She had a smudge of sawdust on her cheek, and though his first inclination was to wipe it off, he looped his thumbs inside his tool belt. "And the overtime Clair is paying the guys hasn't hurt, either. They're highly motivated."

She shook her head. "It's not just the money, it's you. You work right alongside them, never ask anyone to do anything you wouldn't do yourself. Your crew respects that—they respect you. There are things money can't buy, and that's one of them."

Evan stared at Marcy, not sure how to respond. The sincerity in her voice and her big gray-green eyes stunned him. No one had ever said anything like that to him before, except for maybe Jacob. And heck, Jacob was his brother. He had to say stuff like that.

"Thanks." He shrugged, then twisted his head to loosen a knot in his neck. "But I think my men are more concerned about pleasing you than me. In case you haven't noticed, you've got a few fans here, too. I may have to fire James if he doesn't stop staring at you."

Course, then he'd have to fire himself, too, Evan thought.

"James?" Forehead furrowed, Marcy glanced over at the apprentice. Her cheeks turned pink when she saw that the young man was indeed staring at her. "Surely you don't mean that he—"

Her blush deepened, and she looked back at Evan.

"That's exactly what I mean."

"But he's got to be at least five years younger than me," she said, then frowned. "You can't fire him, I'd feel awful if you did and there's no reason to, anyway. Honestly, I assure you, absolutely nothing is going on between us. Nothing at all." She pushed her glasses up her nose. "You wouldn't really fire him, would you? Please tell me you wouldn't."

Well, she was getting awfully worked up worrying about James, Evan thought. Which made him wonder if maybe something might be going on, or maybe she did have a thing for the kid, but was too embarrassed to admit it. Evan cursed his loose tongue. Why the hell did he have to go and put ideas in Marcy's head?

"I won't fire him, okay?" Evan said irritably. "As long as he keeps his mind on his work, his private life, or yours, is none of my business. Now do you think we can get back to work?"

"Of course." Obviously relieved, Marcy picked up a notepad sitting on a stack of two-by-fours. "I made some sketches and a list for the interior-and-exterior garden area. I'll need to order the flowers and plants by tomorrow. Oh, and we'll need to discuss the sprinkler system and the design of the fountain, too. If you want to do that tonight—"

"Fine." When his cell phone rang, he snatched it off his belt and answered it. "Yeah."

Good grief, Marcy thought when Evan practically growled into the phone. What in the world was *his* problem? He'd been moody the past couple of days, and though she realized he'd been working hard, he certainly didn't need to take it out on her.

She watched his expression soften, then his voice lower as he turned away. "Hey, Olivia, what's up?"

Marcy's heart sank. She shouldn't be surprised. At the party last week, the interior designer had certainly made it clear she was interested in Evan. The woman was confident, beautiful and obviously not afraid to go after what she wanted.

And if she hadn't been going after Evan, Marcy might have appreciated all those traits.

"When?" Marcy heard Evan say, then he glanced at his watch. "Okay, I can do that."

When he hung up, he turned back to her, grinning. "Tonight's out. Why don't you spend the evening with

Clair? We can look at your sketches and ideas in the morning."

"Sure." She forced a smile, didn't tell him that she knew Clair had a dinner appointment with the CEO of an oil company who wanted to book a seminar. "Sounds good."

"Great."

Evan looked up at Tom and yelled, "When that beam's in place, knock off for the day. Tom, have the drywallers and brick masons here at six-thirty sharp tomorrow. I want them done and gone in three days."

When he turned back to her, Marcy could see he was anxious to leave.

"Jacob will be around tonight if there's a problem." He plucked the pencil from behind her ear and scribbled on her notepad. "Here's my cell-phone number if you need me."

If she needed him? Hardly! She'd walk naked through the lobby before she'd call him. "I'll be fine."

"I'm sure you will," he said. "But it's probably best if you stay in your room. Take the evening off and relax."

"Sure, I'll do that," she said through gritted teeth. "See you in the morning."

"Right." He tucked the pencil back behind her ear, met her gaze and his grin widened. "See you in the morning."

Clutching her notebook, she watched him walk away, barely holding on to the emotions bubbling under the surface.

Stay in her room? Relax?

Like hell she would.

Enough of being treated like a child, she thought. Enough of hiding out like a frightened kitten.

Enough of the plain, Miss Marcy Pruitt persona.

She'd need help, of course. She was fully aware of her own limitations. And since she couldn't ask Clair for help, that left only one other person she could turn to.

Straightening her shoulders, she headed for the elevators, then pushed the button for the third floor.

Evan came back to his room that night a satisfied man.

Whistling, he stepped off the elevator and headed down the hallway. It was barely ten-thirty and though he should be dog-tired, he was buzzing with energy.

He paused beside Marcy's room, considered knocking to see if she was sleeping. He leaned closer to the door, listening for the sound of female voices or a television.

Nothing.

Just because he was too keyed up to sleep didn't mean he should wake her up. She'd worked tirelessly this past week and had certainly earned a night off.

Still, he did feel a little guilty leaving her tonight. He supposed she had come to rely on him being around, especially after all the time they'd spent together this past week.

Maybe she was still awake, he thought. Reading or watching television. He knocked lightly.

No answer.

Okay, so she probably was asleep. Or maybe she was in the bedroom watching TV and she couldn't hear. He knocked louder.

Still no answer.

He resisted the urge to knock again. If she was sleeping that soundly, he supposed he should just leave her be. There was really no need to wake her up tonight, anyway. He'd see her in the morning.

He glanced at his phone when he went into his room, but the light wasn't blinking. Maybe he should call her. Just to make sure she was all right. She wouldn't even have to get out of bed, he thought, and picked up the phone. She could just say hello, then go right back to sleep.

When Marcy didn't answer, he frowned at the receiver. Good Lord, the woman must sleep like the dead. After five rings, he hung up.

Sighing, he dragged a hand through his hair, then looked around his room. It felt…empty.

Dammit, he missed her.

Well, hell. It was Friday night. A live band played in the Four Winds lounge on the weekends. A little music and a cold beer in an iced mug would be the perfect way to end the day, he decided.

He took a quick shower, pulled on a pair of tan slacks and a black shirt, then was on his way out the door when he stopped and looked at the phone again.

His palms itched, but he shook his head and kept moving.

The lounge was crowded and noisy, the couples on the small dance floor energetic. Evan knew that the weekend live music had been Clair's idea and it had been wildly successful, drawing not only hotel guests, but locals, as well. Clair, who'd been raised to be a Southern socialite and host tea parties and fund-raisers, had proven to be a savvy businesswoman.

Making his way through the throng of people, Evan glanced around the room. A pretty blonde smiled at him and, out of habit, he smiled back, but kept moving. When a cute redhead danced in front of him, gesturing for him to move onto the dance floor with her, he shook his head.

Maybe this hadn't been such a good idea after all, he thought. He really wasn't in the mood for flirting or idle banter tonight. He started to turn around, intending to head back to his room when he spotted Jacob sitting at the bar.

"Hey," Evan yelled over the music as he slid onto the empty bar stool beside his brother. "Does your fiancé know you're hanging out in bars?"

"I'm meeting her here," Jacob yelled back, then signaled the bartender to bring another beer. "She had a meeting that went late."

"A meeting?" Evan stiffened. "Clair wasn't with Marcy tonight?"

Jacob shook his head. "Clair told me Marcy was with you."

He wasn't liking the sound of this at all. "Why did she think that?"

"Marcy left a message on Clair's machine telling her she'd be out all evening. We assumed she was with you."

"She wasn't," Evan said, frowning. "I told her to stay in tonight."

"You *told* her to stay in?"

"Maybe it was more like a strong suggestion." Worried, Evan glanced around the room. He noticed a man sitting with a pretty, shorthaired brunette in a corner booth, tried to remember where he'd seen the man before. "For her own good."

"For *her* own good—" Jacob lifted an eyebrow "—or yours?"

Evan picked up the mug of beer the bartender slid in front of him. "And what the hell is that supposed to mean?"

"You've got it bad for her," Jacob said over the pulsing Latin beat the band had slipped into. "You're the only one who doesn't know it yet. Well, you and James."

Laughing, Evan took a drink of his beer. "Boy, do you have it wrong, I don't have it bad for—" He stopped, then looked sharply at Jacob. "What about James?"

"He's a cute kid, but his light isn't shining all that bright upstairs." Grinning, Jacob sipped his beer. "He told the guys he's going to ask her out."

"Is that so?" He just might be short one crew member tomorrow, Evan thought irritably.

So is that where she was tonight? he wondered. Out

with James? He looked around the room again, but couldn't imagine the kid would bring her here, not only because Marcy wouldn't want to be out where anyone might recognize her, but also because hanging out in bars simply wasn't her style.

For some reason, Evan's attention was drawn back to the man and woman in the booth. Who *was* that guy? Evan watched the man gesture to a cocktail waitress. Whoever he was, he certainly had good taste, Evan thought. The brunette he sat next to was hot, and the little black dress and high heels she wore revealed a pair of legs that went on till Tuesday, not to mention a plunging neckline that showed a generous display of lovely female flesh.

"Hi, guys. Sorry I'm late." Clair slid her hands around Jacob's shoulders, then kissed his cheek and smiled at Evan. "Where's Marcy?"

"Evan lost her," Jacob offered.

"I didn't lose her," Evan said tightly, then stood and gave Clair his stool. "But I will go look for her."

Clair shook her head. "She left a message for me fifteen minutes ago, asking me to meet her in the lounge when I finished my appointment."

"Here?" Evan's gaze shot through the crowd of people again. "Is she crazy? Someone will spot her here, for sure."

"I thought it was a bit odd," Clair said, furrowing her forehead. "There's Sam. Let me go ask him if—ohmigod."

Evan followed the direction of Clair's startled gaze.

She was looking at the man in the corner booth. *Sam.* Her general manager. That's why the guy looked so familiar. And the hottie sitting next to him—

It couldn't be.

Evan stared at the woman in the sexy black dress and high heels. The woman with the wispy, short hair and plunging neckline.

Marcy?

He stared at her, and when her gaze lifted and met his, the corners of her glossy red mouth turned up. He'd know that smile anywhere. And those eyes.

It *was* Marcy.

His heart slammed in his chest.

"Good heavens," Clair breathed. "Well I don't think she has to worry about anyone recognizing her."

"Close your mouth, bro." Jacob slapped a hand on Evan's shoulder. "You're drooling."

"Shut up," Evan growled. But afraid that his brother was right, he snapped his jaw closed.

"Why don't you go say hi?" Jacob suggested.

"I intend to," Clair said. When Jacob grabbed her arm and eased her onto the bar stool, she looked at him. "What?"

"I was talking to Evan," he said, lifting an eyebrow.

"Oh." Clair looked at Evan, then Marcy, then back to Evan. "*Oh.* Right."

"Course, you might not want to bother her." Jacob picked up his beer and slipped an arm around Clair's waist. "Seeing's how she's on a date and all."

Date? A muscle twitched in the corner of Evan's right eye. He leaves her alone for one lousy evening and she not only turns into a sexpot, she's on a date?

He'd see about that.

He slapped his beer back onto the counter, then made his way across the bar.

Seven

Dear Marcy,
I need to replace an arched panel of glass over the windows in my bedroom, but there are so many choices! I'd like something that not only lets the light in, but is romantic and pretty, as well. What do you think will best set the mood?
Caren in Fairfax

Marcy's heart slammed against her ribs when Evan moved through the crowded bar toward her. Good heavens! The intensity in his dark, narrowed gaze sucked the breath right out of her. Her hand tightened on the glass of merlot Sam had bought her. She knew if she'd have been standing, her knees would have buckled under her for certain.

"You okay?" Sam asked.

"Fine," she lied, gulping down a swallow of wine. "Absolutely fine."

"If you're worried about anyone recognizing you, we can—"

"No." If she wasn't so nervous, she'd have laughed. "Even *I* don't recognize me."

"Marcy." Sam smiled and covered her hand with his. "You look incredible. Relax."

It had been awkward at first, asking the Four Winds general manager to help her create a new look for herself. But Sam—and the entire staff at the beauty salon— had been wonderful. For the past five hours, she had been trimmed and polished, waxed and buffed, sculpted and dressed.

Marcy Pruitt was a new woman.

A new, *terrified* woman.

Heart hammering, she watched Evan move closer.

While she'd been sitting in the salon chair, she had told herself it didn't matter what Evan's reaction would be. She told herself she was changing her appearance because *she* wanted to. But she knew that was a lie. She hadn't done this for herself.

She'd done this for Evan.

Maybe it was stupid, maybe it was foolish, but she'd wanted him to look at her exactly the way he was looking at her right now. As if he wanted to consume her.

Sam leaned in and whispered in her ear, "I think it's time for me to go."

"Go?" At the thought of being left alone with Evan,

sheer terror shot up her spine. "But you—we just got here."

Sam glanced at Evan, who was quickly making his way toward their table. "I think we both know who you'd rather have sitting here."

She opened her mouth to protest, but it seemed useless to even attempt to lie. Apparently, Sam hadn't completely bought her story that she'd simply wanted a new look so she wouldn't have to hide in her room the rest of her visit.

With a sigh, she slumped back in her seat. "Am I that obvious?"

"You aren't, but Evan is. And if I want to keep my teeth, I better leave now." Sam looked at Evan again, then grinned. "Oh, what the hell, let's push him to the edge."

It startled Marcy when Sam leaned over and kissed her cheek. When she glanced at Evan, his eyes had narrowed to dark slits.

"Night, Marcy," Sam said, then stood and nodded at Evan. "Mr. Carver."

Evan stopped in front of the table and nodded back. "Sam."

Evan stared bullets at Sam's back when he walked away, then he slid into the booth next to Marcy. "What do you think you're doing?"

"Having a drink with Sam," she said in what she hoped was a casual tone. "At least I was."

"You know what I mean." He frowned at her. "What are you doing, hanging around in a bar, dressed like that? And what did you do to your hair?"

Her heart sank. She'd completely misread him. What a fool she'd been to even hope he might want her if she changed the way she looked. It seemed that even an army of salon technicians couldn't turn plain little Marcy Pruitt into a femme fatale. She was as resistible now as she had been before, only she was killing her feet in the process.

And *that* made her downright grumpy.

"I don't know what your problem is, Evan Carver," Marcy said coolly. "But I happen to like my hair *and* the dress and if I want to hang around in a *bar,* as you so rudely put it, then that is *my* business."

"Did I say I didn't like your hair or the dress?" He stared at her with a look of utter confusion, then sighed heavily. "For God's sake, what's not to like? What I meant was *why* did you do it?"

"I'm sick of hiding in my room, then watching over my shoulder when I do come out." Though the story obviously hadn't worked with Sam, it *was* partially true. "I figured if you and Clair and Jacob didn't recognize me, then I'd be safe."

His frown deepened. "Lady, the last thing you are right now is safe. Come on. We're getting out of here."

"But I haven't finished my—"

He took her by the hand and hauled her from the booth, then pulled her behind him through the crowd. Marcy glanced around the bar, but there was no sign of Clair and Jacob. *Some friends,* she thought, leaving her alone with Evan like this. With no one to rescue her, all she could do was toddle along behind Evan as fast as her ice-pick heels would allow.

Terrific. Her humiliation was complete. He'd probably order cocoa for her and tuck her in bed, although that was one way to get him in her bedroom, she thought.

It surprised her when Evan dragged her not toward the elevators, but outside, where he headed toward the construction site.

"What are you doing?" she managed between breaths.

"I want you to see something."

"Tonight?"

"Tonight."

So much for the new Marcy Pruitt. Apparently, Evan was still more interested in talking business. She might as well be wearing overalls and boots.

He paused at the opening of the heavy plastic liners that enclosed the construction site. "Close your eyes."

"What?"

"Close your eyes."

She sighed, then did as he asked. He took her by the shoulders, then led her through the opening. The air was hot inside, the scent of sawdust heavy. She could hear the sound of rippling water from the nearby fountain, and the faint beat of music coming from a party in one of the ballrooms.

"This is crazy," she muttered, couldn't deny that his hands on her shoulders made her pulse race. She cursed herself for being weak. "You're crazy."

"Yeah." He guided her slowly across the floor. "I think maybe I am. Okay, open your eyes."

She did, then gasped.

Moonlight streamed through the large, beveled and stained-glass window that had been installed high on one wall. The pattern was an intricate diamond cut, with a border of red roses that intertwined with vines of deep green. Over the window, an arched panel continued the diamond cut, with two red roses in the center.

It literally took her breath away.

"How…when…?"

"I had asked Olivia to keep her eyes open for a window," he said. "She found this one at an auction today."

"That's why she called you?" Marcy turned and looked at Evan. "I thought—"

She bit her lip and quickly turned back around.

"What did you think?"

She ignored his question. "Why didn't you tell me what you were doing?"

"I was going to surprise you in the morning."

The moonlight cast a pattern of iridescent diamonds and roses across the walls and stone floor. "It's beautiful."

When his hands slid up her arms and cupped her shoulders, a thrill raced up her back.

"You're beautiful," he said softly.

No man had ever said those words to her before. She

hadn't realized until this moment how badly she'd wanted to hear them. For the first time in her life, she felt like a woman. A desirable, sexy woman.

He'd moved so close their bodies were nearly touching. "What did you think when Olivia called me?" he asked her again.

With his mouth next to her ear, she couldn't even think straight, let alone lie. "I—I assumed you were with—" She hesitated. It was too embarrassing to even say it.

"With Olivia?"

She nodded.

"Marcy, I'm not interested in Olivia."

When his lips brushed her earlobe, her pulse skittered through her veins. "You're not?"

"No." He ran the tip of his finger up her neck. "Your skin feels like rose petals."

His touch sent shivers all the way down to her toes. She closed her eyes and leaned into his chest, felt the warmth of his skin radiate through his shirt.

"I like your hair short," he murmured. "Now I can do this."

He nibbled on the back of her neck and her knees went weak. "That's—" she shuddered when his teeth nipped skin "—nice."

He lifted his head. "Just nice?"

"*Very* nice."

"Marcy," he whispered softly. "I want you."

Her heart leaped. "I—I want you, too."

He turned her in his arms and looked down at her, his gaze somber. "I need you to be sure. If you have any doubts, then just—"

She touched the tips of her fingers to his mouth. "No doubts."

He kissed her fingers, then circled her wrist with his hand and pressed his mouth to her palm. Such a simple touch, yet it made her blood burn. When he bent his head, she slid her hands around his shoulders and pressed closer, parting her lips when his mouth touched hers. His kiss was gentle, but insistent, and when he pulled away, they were both breathing hard.

Desire glinted dark in his eyes. He took her hand and turned. "Let's go."

She hurried after him, struggling to keep up with his long strides. A mix of excitement and nervousness shivered through her, but she wanted this, wanted Evan, with a need she'd never experienced before. Knowing that he wanted her, too, made her heart sing with joy.

His face set with purpose, he led her to the elevators without saying a word. Once they were inside and the doors swished closed, he dragged her into his arms again. His mouth was hungry and hard, and his kisses left her breathless.

"My room." He reached for her hand again when the elevator doors opened.

"Wait." She paused to take off her shoes, then together they hurried down the hall.

She felt giddy and delirious with anticipation. He dropped his room card twice and they were both laughing when he finally managed to get the door open.

He pulled her inside, then dropped his mouth on hers and backed her up against the closed door. She melted against him, returning his kiss, meeting the thrust of his hot tongue with her own.

Her shoes tumbled to the floor.

When his hands slid slowly down her arms and the tips of his thumbs brushed the sides of her breasts, pleasure shot through her like a hot spear.

"You are so damn soft," he said raggedly. "I've wanted to get my hands on you since the minute I met you."

Since the minute I met you? Stunned, she lifted her gaze to his. "You mean before I—before tonight?"

He smiled at her. "Sugarplum, you look sexy as hell, and I'd be lying if I didn't say I love what you've done. But you didn't have to change one little thing for me. Even those overalls you've been wearing all week turned me on."

"My overalls?" She furrowed her forehead. "You're kidding."

"Nope." He ran his lips over hers and nibbled the corner of her mouth. "I couldn't stop thinking about taking them off you."

He meant it, she realized. He really had wanted her before tonight. Had thought about her in her *overalls,* for heaven's sake! His words thrilled and empowered her, brought out the woman in her she hadn't known existed until this moment.

"Well, if you prefer them to this dress," she teased, "I suppose I could go put them on."

"You're not going anywhere, Miss Pruitt," he said, shaking his head. "Except my bed."

She gasped when he swept her up in his arms and headed for the bedroom. She wrapped her arms around his strong shoulders, breathed in the fresh, manly scent of his skin. Salty, she thought, sliding her tongue over a spot directly below his earlobe. Spicy. He sucked in a breath when she explored the area further with her teeth and tongue. It surprised, and pleased her that she could draw that kind of a reaction from him, made her wonder what else she could do...

It would be interesting to find out.

He stopped beside the bed, crushing his mouth to hers as he lowered her to the floor. She wrapped her arms tightly around his neck and clung to him. Sensations spiraled through her, textures, and colors, as brilliant as they were intricate, all swirled together in a vortex of need. This moment, this man; there was nothing else.

Oh, but there *was* something else, she thought dimly when he reached for the zipper on the back of her dress. There was a great deal more.

She shivered with anticipation.

The soft rasp of her zipper mixed with the sounds of their labored breathing. His callused hands skimmed over the sensitive skin on her back; pleasure, intense, shimmering, rippled through her body. Her dress floated slowly down her body, pooled around her bare feet. She stood before him, naked, except for two slivers of black satin.

"I want to see you," he whispered, then inched back and looked down at her.

His gaze seared her, heated her insides, softened her bones. If her knees hadn't locked, she was certain she would have sunk to the floor. She heard Evan's soft hiss as he released a breath, heard him mutter something inaudible. He reached for her, cupped her aching, swollen breasts in his large hands, then caressed the hardened nipples with the pads of his thumbs.

Her head dropped back on a moan, and when he lowered his head and kissed the soft swell of one breast, she bit her bottom lip and sucked in a breath. He took his time, nuzzling, lightly biting her skin. Impatient, eager, she twisted against him, wanting him to hurry. But still he took his time, a lifetime, she thought, until finally his hands moved to the clasp of her bra. It fell away.

His mouth was hot and wet; his tongue stroked. When he drew her nipple in and sucked gently, a sharp arrow of intense pleasure shot from her breast to the V of her legs. She moaned, overpowered by the driving, overwhelming need coursing through her. He took his time, giving equal attention to each breast. With every heated kiss and slide of his hands and tongue, the tension coiled inside her, tighter and tighter, until she thought she could bear it no longer.

"Evan," she gasped, dragging her hands through his thick, dark hair. "Please."

They tumbled to the bed, rolled until he was over her, his hands moving up her thighs, over her hips. The texture of his rough hands on her soft skin was like nothing she'd ever experienced before. She felt wonderfully, gloriously *alive,* as if every nerve ending were exposed, and she shuddered from the intense pleasure rippling over her body.

"Clothes," she murmured, working clumsily at the buttons on his shirt. When the last one opened, he yanked the shirt off, his mouth never leaving hers. Quickly, eagerly, she moved her hands over his solid, broad chest and arms, felt the ripple of sinew and the heat of arousal. She wanted to touch him all over, wanted him to touch her all over. She spread her fingers across his chest, then pressed her lips to his hot skin. His muscles jumped under her touch, and when she slid her hands down his belly to the buckle of his belt and opened it, he drew in a breath.

He moved away from her, quickly tugging off his clothes, and then he was back, his mouth on hers, kissing her hard and deep, until she was dizzy and gasping for breath.

His hand slid to the juncture of her thighs and cupped her; she sank back into the mattress on a moan, and when his finger slipped under the thin sliver of black satin and into the hot, damp glove of her body and stroked her, she writhed under his touch.

She reached for him, closed her hand around the

hard length of his arousal, stunned at the feel of velvet over steel. The longing in her turned to a desperation. She wanted, *needed* him inside her and she stroked him, wanting to pleasure him as he did her.

"Wait." He stilled her hand, then circled her wrist with his fingers. "Not yet."

She wanted to protest, but then his mouth clamped onto her breast and sucked hard. Instinctively, her body bowed upward. His tongue laved her tight, pebbled nipple while his finger continued to stroke between her thighs. She gripped the bedclothes in her fists, felt the cool sheets against her back while fire raced through her blood. And then the sliver of black satin was gone and his mouth moved down her belly. She stilled, shocked at the direction of his roving lips.

"Evan! It's too—I can't—"

But her words were cut off when his lips moved over her, lightly nipping, caressing. When the tip of his tongue found the core of her, she bucked upward, dragging her fingers across his scalp on a gasp.

A person could surely die from pleasure this intense, she thought. Her entire body throbbed, and the pleasure mixed with pain.

"Please," she begged. "Now…"

He lifted his head, blazed kisses across her belly, her hip, then he moved away, left her quivering with need while he dug through the nightstand. And then he was back, lowering himself between her legs, easing himself gently into the heat of her body.

"I don't want to hurt you," he murmured, bracing himself on his forearms.

"You won't." She wound her arms tightly around his shoulders and wrapped her legs over his. "It's wonderful."

Still, he hesitated, and she could see the effort in the tight set of his jaw and narrowed eyes. Sweat beaded on his forehead.

"Just tell me if—"

"Now," she repeated, lifting herself up, moving her hips against his in a sensual rhythm as old as time.

Desire swamped caution, and the need, raw and wild, consumed them both. The urgency built, higher, hotter, tighter, then broke fiercely inside her, his name on her lips when she shattered. His hands on her hips, he held her tightly, his thrusts deep and hard, fast. On a groan, he shuddered violently, again and again.

When he stilled, she slid her arms around his neck to steady herself as much as to draw him closer. The weight of his body pressed her into the mattress. Smiling, she sank into the softness and brought him with her.

"I'm crushing you," Evan said when he could think again, when he could breathe. His heart was still thundering in his head, his lungs burning.

"No." She tightened her hold on him. "Don't move."

He didn't think he had the strength to. No experience had ever left him this spent, this weak, and the best he could manage was to lift his head and gaze down at her.

And feel as if he'd been socked in the gut.

The moonlight played across her face, giving her an ethereal appearance. As he looked at her, he felt something shift in his chest and thicken in his throat.

Beautiful, he thought. She was absolutely beautiful. Her eyes were closed, the corners of her kiss-swollen lips curved into a contented smile. Knowing that he'd put that smile there, he couldn't stop the smug satisfaction sprinting through his veins.

"Are you okay?" he asked quietly.

Her eyes slowly fluttered open. "If you have to ask, I must have done something wrong."

"You know what I mean." He kissed the tip of her nose. "And trust me, you sure as hell didn't do anything wrong. That's about as right as it gets."

"It *was* pretty amazing." Smiling, she ran her fingertips over his shoulders. "Is it always like that?"

It's never been like that, was his first thought, though he couldn't exactly define what was different about making love with Marcy. And some things he simply preferred not to analyze. "You're amazing."

Her smile widened, then she dropped her gaze. "I never thought I'd be any good at it."

"Why on earth would you think that?"

"I always figured there was something wrong with me because I was more interested in my work than in dating or sex. I'd hear other women talk about it, but I never could really understand what all the hoopla was about. And now—" she raked her fingers lightly across his back "—well, now, I do."

The light rake of her fingernails on his skin and the upward thrust of her hips made his heart slam in his chest. He clamped his hands on her hips and rolled to his back, bringing her with him. Eyes wide, she gasped at the unexpected movement.

"I've heard it called many things." He slid his hands up her sides, then cupped her pretty breasts in his hands, watched her gaze darken with desire again. "But never a hoopla."

Chuckling, she covered his hands with her own, then the smile faded from her mouth as she found her rhythm. He'd never seen anything more arousing than the sight of her moving over him, her lips softly parted, her eyes clouded with need.

"You know," she said, her voice breathless, "you called a six-thirty start tomorrow."

"Thinking about work?"

"Just wondering how late I can keep you up." Her eyes widened as she realized what she'd said. "I mean, awake."

Laughing softly, he thrust his hips up to meet hers. "Why don't we find out?"

Eight

Dear Marcy,
I loved your article on diet and nutrition in your
March issue. Do you have any other suggestions
for cutting calories and getting in shape?
Jeannie in Cortland

Every muscle in her body ached when Marcy woke at 5 a.m. She wasn't certain she could move, let alone get out of bed, get dressed and walk across the hall to her own room.

She hadn't intended to stay the night, had even tried to leave at 2 a.m., then again at three. But each time Evan had dragged her back into his arms, and each time he'd changed her mind.

Not that she'd put up much of a fight.

She looked at the man sleeping soundly beside her. He lay on his stomach, one muscled arm wrapped around a pillow, the other arm draped possessively across her waist. Even in sleep he looked tough and rugged and absolutely virile.

Even in sleep he made her tingle all over.

After the night they'd spent together, she wouldn't have thought she'd had any tingle left in her. Evan had been an amazing lover. Tender and gentle one moment, then lusty and demanding the next.

What shocked, and delighted her, was that she'd been equally lusty. Equally demanding.

Who would have ever thought?

No one, she thought. Least of all herself. And the wonder of it left her positively in awe. And absolutely thrilled.

There were no regrets. She believed in fate. Believed that whatever happened in life was meant to be. She'd waited for the right moment, for the right man. Last night was the moment; Evan was the man.

She studied his face in the dim light, resisted the urge to run her fingertips over the dark shadow of his morning beard. And it wasn't just his face she wanted to touch. She wanted to explore every inch of solid muscle, every hard plane and sharp angle of masculine physique. Curiosity might have killed the cat, she thought, but she would certainly die one happy cat.

Desperately, she tried not to confuse the physical act of making love with the emotional feeling of love. But lying here, her body still humming from the most incredible night of her life, the line between the two was hazy. In the light of day, perhaps, that line would be more distinct. But there was no future for them; she was certain of that, and it would be very foolish to let herself fall in love with Evan.

She didn't have the experience to know how to act now, or what to say. When she thought about what they'd shared last night, what they'd done, her cheeks burned. Maybe it would be easier if she wasn't here when he woke. Isn't that what men always said they wanted? Space? She could give him that.

Holding her breath, she slowly, quietly, eased herself from under his arm, then sat on the edge of the bed and reached for her dress.

"Get back here."

She jumped at the sound of his raspy voice, didn't have time to respond before his hand snaked out and dragged her back into bed with him.

"It's five o'clock," she argued, then gasped when he rolled and pinned her underneath him.

"Yeah?" He rubbed his lips lightly over hers. "So?"

"You have to be—"

"Right here." He nuzzled the corner of her mouth. "And right here."

When he blazed feather-light kisses across her jaw, then down her neck, she sighed. When he nibbled on her shoulder, she shivered.

"Right there is nice, too," she said breathlessly.

He took his time, moving his mouth over her, gently biting, tasting, until she was floating on a soft cloud of sensual pleasure.

When his mouth moved to her breasts, the cloud

turned thick and heavy, darkening with every brush of his lips and every slide of his tongue. She arched upward when he sucked strongly on her nipple, moved her hips against his. When he kneed her thighs apart, then slid inside her, she groaned.

She murmured his name, met every thrust of his hips, wrapped her arms and legs tightly around him. The urgency grew, higher and hotter, coiling tighter, then tighter still.

The climax rolled through her, then broke apart. She cried out, raking her nails across the rippling muscles of his broad shoulders. He thrust harder, deeper, then moaned, shuddered with the force of his climax.

Her arms slid bonelessly to her sides. She wasn't sure how much time had passed before she was able to think again. If she'd had the strength, she might have glanced at the bedside clock.

As her senses returned, she heard the sound of Evan's harsh breathing and felt the wild beating of his heart. He lay sprawled on top of her, heavy, but not uncomfortable.

"Wow," he murmured, rubbing his lips across her jaw.

She smiled. It was the sweetest, most wonderful thing any man had ever said to her.

"Yeah." She found the strength to slide her hands up his arms. "Wow."

He raised himself on his elbows and gazed down at her. "You are the damnedest woman, Miss Pruitt."

She traced a fingertip over his chin. "I hope that's a compliment."

"Oh, yeah." He kissed her fingertips. "It's a compliment."

"Thank you," she said primly, then drew in a sharp breath when he slid his hands down her sides and cupped her breasts. "By the way—" she struggled to pull air into her lungs "—I agree with your reasoning to go into the construction business instead of the sciences."

"Oh?" He circled her nipples with the pads of his thumbs and she squirmed, was shocked at the rush of desire coursing through her. "And what reason was that?"

"You really are very, very good with your hands."

Evan did his best not to whistle when he walked onto the job site later that morning. The last thing he needed was to draw any unwanted attention from his men, and the fact that he was more than an hour late would already raise a few eyebrows. If he showed up in a good mood, as well, he'd be the subject of intense scrutiny, not to mention a great deal of ribbing.

But hell, he *was* the boss here, he reasoned. As long as the work got done, he could be as late as he wanted— although he might never have shown up at all if he'd done what he wanted.

It was damn hard to leave a sexy, naked woman in his bed.

He'd told Marcy to stay in and get some sleep, that there really wasn't anything she needed to do until after the drywall was up and they looked at paint samples. But his motive for suggesting she sleep in had been entirely selfish. He couldn't wait to get the woman back in bed tonight, and he wanted her well rested when he did.

He'd certainly been right about one thing. Marcy's enthusiasm and creativity had carried over into the bedroom.

He still wasn't sure exactly what had happened last night. Well, other than the fact that they'd made love. Several times, he thought, smiling. But something else had taken place, too. Something that went beyond simple pleasure. He'd hardly been a monk in his life, but he'd never experienced anything like this before. Never experienced anything like Marcy.

The intensity. The near insanity. The overwhelming desperation. It was all new to him. It made him edgy and yet exhilarated at the same time.

"You should probably wipe that grin off your face," Evan heard Jacob say from behind him. "The men are already taking bets as to who the lucky lady was last night."

When Evan turned, Jacob held out a tall, steaming mug of coffee. Frowning, Evan took the mug. "Don't mess with me, bro. It's too damn early."

"I'm not messing with you."

Evan looked at his crew, who were all staring at him. When he scowled at them, they all quickly turned back to their work.

"Nobody looks that happy in the morning unless they got—"

"Shut up." Evan lowered his voice when a few men glanced over. "It wasn't like that."

"So what was it then?"

"None of your damn business," Evan said irritably.

"Normally, I'd agree with you," Jacob said evenly. "But we're talking about a woman's reputation here, and she's one of Clair's best friends, too."

Jacob was right, Evan thought with a sigh. He just wasn't used to explaining himself to anyone. "I like her. That's what this is. She's smart and sweet and there's nothing phony about her. She's…different from any other woman I've ever been with before."

"To say the least," Jacob said with a nod. "She's also more vulnerable."

"You think I don't know that?" Evan shot back, then dragged a hand through his hair. "Why the hell do you think I've kept my hands off her this long? But it happened, and I'm not sorry it did. And I can tell you right now, it's going to happen again."

"You're both adults." Jacob folded his arms. "All I'm asking is for you to be careful."

"I am being careful," he said, letting his temper ease off. "She's the last person I want to see get hurt. But we happen to enjoy each other's company, so until she goes back to Los Angeles, that's the way it is."

"Is that so?"

"That's what I said, didn't I?" Evan didn't like the look in Jacob's eyes. One of those big-brother, I-know-something-you-don't looks. "Now if you're through interrogating me, do you think we can get to work?"

"Uh, boss?"

James stood a few feet away, shifting awkwardly. Evan glared at the young man, hoped he hadn't heard the exchange between Jacob and himself. "What?"

"Uh, do you know where Marcy is?"

Talk about bad timing. Part of Evan wanted to say *yeah, she's in my bed, now buzz off and don't even think about looking at her again.* But the part of his brain that was still managing to operate properly took control. "Why do you want to know?"

"Well, there was an inspector here asking about her a while ago."

"Inspector?" Evan narrowed his gaze. "What inspector?"

"Tall guy, thick glasses, hard hat and clipboard. Said he was from Building and Safety, and that she'd asked him about a code spec."

Evan looked at Jacob, saw the concern in his brother's eyes. "Do you know anything about this?"

Jacob shook his head. "I just got here ten minutes ago."

Evan was as sure as he could be that Marcy hadn't called or even spoken to Building and Safety about a code spec. He wasn't liking the sound of this one little bit. "He asked specifically for Marcy Pruitt?"

"I think so." James scratched his neck. "Or maybe he didn't. Gosh, now I'm not sure."

Evan clenched his jaw. "And what did you tell him?"

James grinned. "I told him I didn't know who he was talking about."

Thank God. Evan released the breath he'd been holding. "All right, but if you see this guy again, let me know."

"Sure thing." James shoved his hands into the front pockets of his jeans. "So, ah, *do* you know where she is?"

Evan narrowed a look at James. "Get your butt back to work or you're fired."

"But—"

"Now," Evan barked.

"Sure, boss."

Evan glared at James's back as he scurried away.

"Well, that was subtle," Jacob said, shaking his head.

"Tell Tom I'll be gone for a while." Evan took off the tool belt he'd just strapped on. "You keep an eye out for anyone hanging around who shouldn't be."

Dammit! Evan turned and headed back toward the elevators. If he hadn't been late, he'd have been here when the guy had shown up. And if he hadn't really been an inspector, Evan thought, he'd have given the man something to look for, all right—his teeth.

But now, Evan was more concerned about Marcy than putting his fist in some jerk's face. He needed to know she was all right. The image of her lying in his bed, those long legs of hers entwined in the rumpled sheets, her hair tousled and her cheeks flushed, quickened more than his pace.

Hopefully—he glanced at his wristwatch as he pushed the elevator button—the woman would be right where he'd left her.

* * *

The Four Winds coffee shop had the same casual finesse as the rest of the hotel. Mirrored walls, soft leather booths, fresh flowers. In spite of the early hour, several tables were occupied by hotel guests, but no one seemed to notice Marcy as she followed a cheerful, gray-haired hostess to a corner booth where Clair was already seated. It felt good, Marcy thought, to walk in a public place and not have people stare at her. Although, as she glanced around the restaurant, she did notice a nice-looking man watching her over the newspaper he was reading.

The attention gave her an extra shot of confidence, but she wasn't interested in any man other than Evan. She knew she was walking around with a silly grin on her face, but she couldn't help herself. It was all she could do to keep herself from skipping across the restaurant.

Her smile widened when she slipped into the booth with Clair and gave her a quick hug. "Thank you so much for meeting me."

"You're kidding, right?" Clair slid a cup of steaming coffee across the table toward Marcy. "Jacob had to hold me back from calling you at six. Look at you, my God! You look amazing. And your hair—I love it!"

Smiling, Marcy touched the short ends at the back of her neck. They were still damp from her rushed shower, but all the cut required was a quick blow-dry and a simple finger comb. Her face felt naked without her glasses, but she'd taken the time to brush on some pink lip gloss and a touch of mascara—something she wouldn't have bothered to do before today.

When she glanced in the mirrored wall, she still didn't recognize the woman staring back.

"It's going to take some getting used to," she said, looking back at Clair. "But I like it, too. Your salon staff are all magicians."

"They're good, granted, but they had a great subject to work with." Clair scooted in closer. "Now you want to tell me what possessed you to take a multimillion-dollar image and change it?"

"My hair will grow back." With what she hoped was a casual shrug, Marcy picked up a menu. "I was just tired of hiding out and looking over my shoulder all the time." She used the exact same words she'd said to Evan last night. "I figured if you and Jacob and Evan couldn't recognize me, then no one else will, either."

Clair gave her the same doubtful look that Evan had. "You're saying you did this because you didn't want anyone to recognize you?"

Without her glasses, Marcy had to bring the menu a little closer than normal. "Of course."

"Marcy." Clair pushed the menu back down with her finger. "Sorry, hon, but you never were a very good liar. And I'm not blind. I saw the look in Evan's eyes when he dragged you out of the lounge last night. You want to tell me what that was all about?"

Marcy tightened her grip on the menu. Why had she thought she could hide the truth from Clair, when even Sam had seen through her? Drawing in a breath to steady her nerves, she closed her menu and met Clair's gaze. "We…slept together."

"Well, duh." Clair rolled her eyes. "I can see that."

Feeling as if all eyes in the restaurant were staring at her, Marcy quickly glanced around, breathed a sigh of relief when she realized no one was watching. Not even the man who'd been reading his newspaper. Now he was staring at a pretty blonde who'd slipped into a booth next to his. Fickle man, she thought with a smile, then looked back at Clair. "What do you mean, you can see?"

"Honey, you're glowing, and when you walked through the restaurant, you looked like you wanted to hug every person here. Trust me, I know that look."

Well, so much for her weak attempt at being nonchalant, Marcy thought. But why was she trying to be casual about the most wonderful night of her life, anyway? Clair was the one person—probably the only person—that Marcy knew she could trust implicitly. Who better to share her joy with?

"Actually," Marcy said quietly, then leaned in closer and smiled slowly, "I felt like skipping."

"Skipping?" Clair arched an eyebrow and picked up a glass of water. "Now *that* sounds serious."

"Oh, not at all," Marcy said, shaking her head. "It's just sex."

"Marcy!" Water sloshed over the sides of Clair's water glass. "I can't believe you just said that."

"Me, either." She laughed at herself, and the look of shock on Clair's face. "But I'm in too good of a mood to be embarrassed. Evan and I might have slept together, but it was just one night, sort of a culmination of all the time we've been spending together."

"That's an understatement." Clair blew out a breath. "So that's it? You're telling me you had a one-night stand with my fiancé's brother and you're fine with that?"

She picked up her coffee and sipped. "Absolutely."

"And you're also saying it's not going to happen again?"

"I really haven't thought that far ahead." Nor could she allow herself to. If making love with Evan was just "one of those crazy, wild nights," then she'd at least have that to take home with her. The last thing she wanted was for Evan to feel awkward around her. And she didn't want him to think that she had any expectations. That would certainly send him running in the opposite direction as fast as his truck and trailer would take him.

"I need to sit down," Clair said, blinking slowly. "Wait. I am sitting down."

Marcy smiled. "I'm still trying to absorb it all myself. But whatever happens, I promise it won't effect Evan's and my working on the chapel. And at the speed Evan's men are moving along, it should be finished in just a few days. You've already got your flowers ordered and I can get the garden area planted easily and, oh-migod, I haven't told you about the stained-glass window yet, you won't believe—"

"Marcy," Clair said quietly, but with emphasis. "Stop already. I'm not worried about the chapel. I'm worried about you."

"Me? Why?"

"Honey, I don't want to see you get hurt."

"Believe me, I've given that a great deal of thought." It was all she could do *not* to think about it. "I'm certain that as long as Evan and I can stay friends, then our relationship doesn't have to be awkward, now or later."

"Friends." Dazed, Clair leaned back in her seat. "You really believe that?"

"I know there are risks," Marcy said softly. "What's life without them? I've been sheltered most of my life, first by my aunt, then by Helen. You of all people know what that's like. But when you ran out of that church, you took a risk. If you had known then that everything between you and Jacob would end badly, would you have done anything differently?"

Clair sighed, then shook her head. "Not one single thing."

"So there you go." Smiling, Marcy covered Clair's hand. "Now can we order food? I'm absolutely starving. Did you know that just kissing for thirty minutes can burn twenty-eight calories? And when you—"

"Dammit, Marcy, where the hell have you been?"

She'd been so engrossed in her conversation with Clair, Marcy hadn't noticed Evan come into the restaurant. Arms folded, he stood beside the table, his eyes narrowed.

"What do you mean, where have I been?" Confused by his behavior, she stared at him. "I've been right here."

"You were supposed to be sleeping," he said tightly. "Why didn't you tell me where you'd be?"

She frowned at him. "I didn't know I needed to."

He slid onto the seat beside her, shocked her when he dropped a kiss on her lips. "Well, you do. Mornin', Clair."

"Morning, Evan." Clair cleared her throat, then pushed her coffee aside. "Ah, maybe I should get to work."

Somber, Evan shook his head. "No, stay."

It struck Marcy that Evan wasn't angry, he was worried. "Is there a problem?" she asked.

"I'm not sure." Evan picked up Marcy's coffee cup and drank from it. "Did you call or speak to anyone at Building and Safety about any code specs?"

She thought about his question. "I know I didn't call, but I suppose it's possible I might have spoken to one of the inspectors at the site. I really wouldn't know if they were with Building and Safety or part of the crew. Why?"

"James said someone was asking about you this morning." He looked at Clair. "Has your staff noticed anyone hanging around who shouldn't be?"

Clair shook her head. "No, but I'll call a staff meeting later and let everyone know to be extra cautious." She glanced at her watch. "I'll also go over all the check-ins for the past few days and see if anyone looks suspicious. If someone knew Marcy was at this hotel, it would make sense they'd stay here, too."

Evan nodded. "Sounds good. And maybe while you're at it, you should change her room. Just in case she's already been spotted. Better yet, she can move her things into my room."

"What!" With great effort, Marcy jumped into a conversation that was already moving at warp speed. "Stop. Both of you. Just stop."

When both Clair and Evan stared at her, waiting, she swallowed, then squared her shoulders. "I don't need to move anywhere. You're both making assumptions, and anyway, even if someone was looking for Marcy Pruitt, do you think he'd recognize me now? The two of you didn't even know who I was last night."

"I suppose that's true," Clair said hesitantly.

Evan frowned. "Maybe, but nevertheless, I'll feel better if you move her into my room."

"*You'll* feel better?" Marcy pressed her lips together and arched an eyebrow. "How about you ask me how *I* feel about that?"

Evan's frown darkened. "Fine. How do you feel about that?"

She took her coffee cup from Evan's hands, then sipped as she looked at Clair. "I'll move my things this morning."

Nine

Dear Marcy,
Help! There are too many choices for wedding hair accessories. Combs and clips, jeweled hair sticks, barrettes, hairpins, tiaras. I know it's a personal choice, but I simply can't decide. What do you suggest?
Arlene in Alabama

With the drywall up and the first coat of mud on, Evan sent his crew home for the day and knocked off early himself. At the rate they were going, the chapel would easily be finished by early next week and that would give them one more week to take their time with the details or any problems that might still arise.

There'd been a camaraderie on this project unlike any he'd ever seen before. Partly because his crew all knew Jacob and liked him, but Evan was sure it was mostly because his men had wanted to please Marcy.

The fact that she hadn't shown up today had caused concern, but Evan had reassured everyone that she was fine and she'd be back tomorrow.

Moving her out of her suite and into his made sense, Evan reassured himself as he rode up the elevator. If this P.I. had managed to track her down to the Four Winds, then it would look as if she'd checked out. Even if the guy was still hanging around, the odds of him recognizing the new Marcy Pruitt were pretty slim. And if he kept her close, Evan reasoned, it would be easier to watch for anyone who might be watching her.

And besides, she'd spent more time in his suite than her own these past few days, anyway. They were both adults, two people mutually attracted to each other. Now that they were sleeping together, why have two rooms when one would do just as well?

Still, it *had* been an impulsive decision. He knew Jacob was right, that Marcy's inexperience with men made her vulnerable. Which was exactly why he probably shouldn't have asked her to move into his room, Evan thought. He cared about Marcy. Probably more than any other woman he'd been with before. He'd chew nails and swallow them before he'd see her hurt.

Damn. He stepped off the elevator and headed for his room. Maybe he hadn't thought this through very well. Maybe it wasn't such a hot idea, after all. He felt a tightening around his throat, then wiped at the fine layer of sawdust on his temple. Maybe he should talk to her. Give her an out now, before things got more—what was the word she'd used herself? Complicated.

He stepped into the room, smiled when he heard the sound of her quietly singing in the bedroom, then moved to the door. The first thing he noticed was the pile of shopping bags on the bed. The second thing he noticed was her.

She stood in front of the closet-door mirrors, wearing a soft pink slip dress. The hem of the dress skimmed her calves, but when she swiveled her hips, the flared skirt danced around her knees.

Damn.

He took in the sight of her long legs, her slender neck and graceful arms. He had to grab hold of the doorjamb to brace himself. There was a lump in his throat, a mixture of lust and fear and something else he couldn't identify. He swallowed hard, and when his brain cleared, managed to catch a few words of what she was singing: …*never gonna get it, never gonna get it*…

"Never gonna get what?"

Clutching her throat, she spun on a gasp. "Evan!"

He stayed where he was, partly because his legs were still locked into place, partly because he was afraid he'd have to touch her if he moved any closer.

"Nice dress."

"Thank you." Her cheeks were a deeper shade of pink than her dress. "I didn't hear you come in."

"Just got here." Lord, she looked pretty in pink. It was all he could do not to put his work-dirty hands on her and gobble her up. "Looks like you went shopping."

"I did. Well, we did." She moved to the bed and picked up a blouse lying there, held it to her chest to cover herself. "Clair has a great boutique here at the hotel, plus we went out to a couple of dress shops in town."

He understood she was modest, but considering the night they'd spent together, it was a little late to hide that lovely body of hers from him. "Looks like you're going to need another suitcase."

"Maybe." She looked at all the clothes. "Or maybe I'll just get rid of what I brought."

"Really?" He leaned against the doorjamb, watched the hem of her skirt flitter around her calves as she shifted awkwardly back and forth. "So you're keeping this new Marcy?"

"I'm thinking about it." She glanced in the mirror at herself, then looked back at him. "What do you think?"

It startled him when his first thought was that *he'd* like to keep her. He shook that thought off and smiled at her. "You looking for a compliment?"

"What if I am?"

When one corner of her mouth curved up and she tossed the blouse back on the bed, his heart jumped into his throat. Another side of her he hadn't see before, he thought—the tease.

He definitely liked it.

He moved toward her and took her hand in his. The texture of her soft, smooth skin against his rough, dust-covered palm absolutely floored him.

"This is what I think." He placed her hand on his chest. "That's what you do to me when I look at you."

His heart was pounding like a bass drum under her fingertips. He watched her catch her bottom lip with her teeth, then smile shyly at him. "Me, too," she said.

"I told you the truth last night, Marcy." He brought her hand to his mouth and pressed his lips to her palm. "You got to me the first time I laid eyes on you. You were so damn cute in that silly hat, so flustered trying not to lie to those women. Makes me laugh every time I think about it."

She stared at him with a mixture of wonder and amazement in her smoky-green eyes. "I—I'm not even going to pretend to know what to say to that."

"You don't have to say anything." When he kissed her wrist, he felt her pulse flutter under his fingertips. "Just stand right there while I go take the world's fastest shower."

"I won't move," she said, her voice breathless.

He started for the bathroom, reached the doorway, then swung around on his heels and came back to her.

"On second thought," he said, grabbing her hand and pulling her to the bathroom with him, "let's make it a nice, long shower. Together."

Sometime later when they were lying in his bed, incapable of movement, Evan realized that he'd completely forgotten about the talk he'd intended to have with Marcy. The one where he would give her an out if she really didn't want to stay in his room. The talk about how maybe they shouldn't complicate their relationship any more than they already had. The talk about how he didn't want her to get hurt.

It was no longer an issue, he decided. She was staying with him and he didn't want to give her an out. And as far as their relationship getting complicated, it was way too late to prevent that.

He still didn't want to hurt her, of course. But who was to say he would? He'd made it clear he wasn't looking to settle down. She was a big girl and they were both adults. They'd tried to deny their attraction and that sure as hell hadn't worked. For the next two weeks, why shouldn't they simply enjoy each other?

Why not indeed? he thought, and tucked her warm body closer to his. With a sigh, she snuggled against him, then drifted off to sleep.

Yeah. He closed his eyes and smiled.

Why not indeed.

"My baby. My beautiful baby." Josephine Beauchamp slipped the last pin into her daughter's veil, then stepped back and clasped her hands to her chest. "Isn't she the most beautiful bride you've ever seen?"

"Mother, please, enough," Clair complained. "You've asked Marcy at least ten times already."

"She does look beautiful," Marcy agreed, and it was true, of course. With her hair pulled back to set off her exotic looks, and the heart-shaped neckline of her beaded gown, Clair was truly a vision in white. "And so do you, Mrs. Beauchamp."

Josephine was a stunning woman, Marcy thought. She looked at least ten years younger than her fifty years and had a figure a thirty-year-old would kill for. Shiny black hair, high cheekbones, deep, blue eyes that matched her designer silk suit—no one would have ever guessed she wasn't Clair's birth mother.

"Thank you, Marcy. And you—" Josephine touched Marcy's cheek and smiled. "Absolutely exquisite."

When Josephine turned back to fuss with Clair's veil, Marcy relaxed. It still made her uncomfortable when anyone complimented her. Not that she hadn't appreciated all the kind words she'd heard over the past few days. She'd enjoyed it immensely. In her entire twenty-six years, she'd never once been whistled at, but when she'd returned to the work site with her new haircut and no glasses, there had been several whistles. When the men realized who she was, the whistles were followed by a long, stunned silence, then a round of applause, then more whistles. Though they'd made her blush, she hadn't minded the attention, but Evan certainly had. He nearly burst a vein when he yelled for everyone to get back to work. At that point, it hadn't taken a genius for everyone—including James—to figure out that she and Evan were sleeping together.

Even to herself, it seemed odd she didn't mind the crew knowing about her and Evan. She wasn't ashamed, and she wasn't embarrassed. She was deliriously happy.

She was hopelessly in love.

It was a mistake, falling in love with Evan. She'd known that from the beginning, had listed all the reasons to remain objective in their relationship, even after they'd shared a bed.

Unfortunately, logic did not exist in the heart. She'd given her feelings flight, and for what felt like a brief, exhilarating moment, she'd soared higher than she could have ever imagined. She wouldn't regret that, not ever.

Tomorrow afternoon she would board a plane for Los Angeles. The day after that, she would be back to work.

Back to reality. Back to the real world.

But if lying in Evan's arms, making love with him, laughing, working, even just sitting on the sofa watching TV—if all that wasn't reality, if that wasn't real, then why did it suddenly hurt so bad?

She wouldn't think about it now. Today was Clair and Jacob's day. Today she would smile and be happy for them. She would enjoy her last day here with her friends and her last evening with Evan. Cherish each and every moment.

A quick knock at the door, then Julianna stuck her head in. "We're good to go out here," she said, smiling at Clair. "You ready?"

"Ready," Clair said, excitement sparkling in her eyes. "Let's do it."

While a string quartet entertained the waiting guests, Evan stood at the front of the crowded chapel, clenching his jaw to distract himself from the bow tie squeezing his throat. How the hell did they expect a guy to even breathe in this monkey suit? he wondered. He figured if he turned blue, he'd at least match the color of the bridesmaids' dresses.

To Evan's left, Rand, Lucas and Seth had assumed the position of groomsmen, as well, and to Evan's right, the groom himself stood as rigid as the beam resting fifteen feet over his head, the same beam that Jacob had helped set in place just two weeks ago.

It amazed Evan that they'd finished with four days to spare, plenty of time for Marcy to add the finishing touches: lush ferns, bubbling wall fountain, oak pews salvaged from an abandoned church and refurbished, a five-foot bronze statue of an angel. Shoot, even *he* would want to be married here, he thought, then quickly frowned.

Figuratively speaking, of course.

Evan stretched his neck to allow more air through his windpipe, then glanced at the wedding guests. Over the past couple of weeks, especially since the incident at the work site, it had become a habit to search the faces around him to look for anyone who might be watching Marcy. But considering the way she'd changed her appearance, watching the people watching Marcy had become a full-time job.

He almost wished she'd kept her old look. At least that way he wouldn't have to walk around with the urge to start a fight with nearly every male who came within twenty feet of her. He'd never had an issue with jealousy before. What the hell was happening to him?

She'd gotten under his skin, dammit. He wasn't even sure how it had happened, or exactly when, but it had. On the job site he found himself constantly seeking her out, and when she wasn't there, he wondered what she was doing. She consumed his thoughts, and it was downright irritating.

They hadn't talked about it, but he knew she had a flight back to Los Angeles tomorrow. She hadn't asked him to take her to the airport; he hadn't offered. Not because he didn't want to drive her, but because he didn't want her to go.

He knew she had to leave, knew he had to be on the road himself. His next project was scheduled to break ground on Tuesday. It wasn't as if either one of them had a choice. But somehow that didn't make it any easier, and the persistent tug in his chest worried him. Even if she was different from any other woman, even if he cared about her more than he had any other woman, that didn't mean he couldn't let her go. He could, dammit.

Just not yet.

When the quartet switched to Handel's *Water Music,* Evan straightened. They'd been given instructions at the rehearsal last night as to who went where when, but he'd had a hard time paying attention. Marcy had worn that pretty pink dress, and all he'd been able to think about was the afternoon he'd taken it off her. And then all he'd been able to think about was taking it off her again.

When they'd gotten back to their room last night, that was exactly what he'd done. The memory of what had happened next made him smile. All that silky smooth skin under his hands…the sound of soft laughter when he'd kissed that ticklish spot on her ribs…her sigh when he'd slid into her…

Good grief. He blinked, reminded himself that he was standing in front of one hundred and fifty people—fantasizing about Marcy!

Thankfully, every head in the room had already turned to watch Julianna emerge from the back of the chapel. Grace followed several steps behind, then Hannah. Carrying small bouquets of white roses, they all wore blue satin that flowed to their ankles. No doubt about it, Evan thought as he watched the women walk up the aisle. The Blackhawk family had some fine-looking females.

And then Marcy stepped through the doorway and the other women blurred from his vision.

He went numb.

Her dress was the same color blue, but unlike the others, it was strapless, emphasizing her long neck and lovely shoulders. Diamonds sparkled on her earlobes and at the base of her throat. Her smile lit up the room. When she turned her smoky-green gaze on him, he swore his heart stopped.

He was certain if someone even blew on him, he'd fall straight back.

His pulse pounded as she walked down the aisle, then up the steps toward him. She took her place beside the other women and he slowly released the breath he'd been holding, then waited for the feeling to come back into his body. When the bridal march began, Evan heard the gasps and murmurs of delight, then turned to watch Clair walk down the aisle. She looked beautiful, of course, and happy. Evan glanced at Jacob, saw the moisture in his brother's eyes as he watched his bride glide closer to him. Evan had to clear his throat.

Since they'd been kids, he and Jacob had only had each other to rely on. Now Jacob had Clair, and though Evan knew all their lives would be better, he also knew they'd be different.

He was happy for them both, yet he suddenly felt as if part of him was being torn away, leaving a jagged, empty hole. He shrugged the feeling off, told himself all this hearts-and-flowers stuff was making him soft and he'd be glad when it was over.

He glanced at Marcy, felt the hole in his chest widen and knew there was one thing he wasn't glad about.

When Clair's father handed her to Jacob, Evan squared his shoulders and turned his attention to the reason they were all *really* here, of course.

Free beer and food.

Lights twinkled in every darkened corner of the Four Winds ballroom. Huge floral arrangements, white and blue, graced every table. Silverware clinked against fine china. The food was impeccable, the champagne as expensive as it was endless.

But it was the bride and groom who stole the show, Marcy thought, watching Clair and Jacob gaze into each other's eyes while they danced together on the crowded floor. It was impossible to imagine two people more in love.

Until she'd met Evan, Marcy couldn't have even guessed what it felt like.

She sat at a table, her shoes off, watching Evan as he scooped up Julianna and Lucas's little girl in his arms and danced with her. The child laughed when he dipped her and Marcy found herself laughing, too, even while her heart ached.

I'll get over him, she told herself. Maybe fall in love again. It could happen.

In another lifetime, maybe.

She let herself feel the pain for a moment, then pushed it away. There would be plenty of time for that later, she told herself. Too much time.

"I think there's a law here against not dancing." Rand sat in the chair next to her. "That's what my wife told me, anyway."

Marcy tilted her head. "You're not dancing."

"The boys sent me on a beer run. Can I get you anything?"

"No, thanks." She held up the glass of champagne she'd been sipping. "I'm good."

Apparently in no hurry to complete his beer mission,

Rand settled back in the chair. "I hear you're headed back to L.A. tomorrow."

She nodded. "As it is, I've been gone so long my manager had to double her antianxiety medication."

"Send her out here," Rand said. "Nothing like mucking out a stall or riding fence to reduce stress. I could use another hand."

Just the thought of Helen mucking out a stall or riding a horse made Marcy laugh. With her manicured nails, designer suits and expensive shoes, Helen Dunbar was the last woman in the world to wield a pitchfork or ride a horse. "I'll be sure and extend your offer."

"You do that." Grinning, Rand stretched out his long legs. "So I take it nothing ever came of her hiring a P.I. to find you."

"Jacob's friend in L.A. couldn't find anything, and my assistant, Anna, never heard Helen mention it again. It seems we all overreacted." Marcy smiled when Evan scooped up Hannah's twin girls and somehow managed to dance with all three children. "And even if she did hire someone to find me, it doesn't matter now, anyway. Obviously, they didn't."

"By the way—" Rand glanced at the dance floor, then looked back at Marcy "—that was a nice toast Evan gave."

"It was, wasn't it?" she said with a smile. Evan had made everyone laugh when he'd asked for all of Jacob's old girlfriends to return his house keys and at least a dozen women, including one of the female servers and Clair's mother, stood up and handed over keys. Then he'd made everyone sigh when he'd raised his glass and welcomed Clair Carver to the family.

But Evan hadn't been the only brother-in-law to propose a toast to the newlyweds. Rand had stood up, as well. "Your toast was beautiful, Rand," Marcy said. "You made Clair cry."

"I got a little choked up myself," Rand admitted, then frowned at Marcy. "But if you tell anyone I said that, I'll deny it."

Marcy smiled. In fact, there hadn't been a dry eye in the house after Rand had stood and said that Clair might be Jacob's wife, but she would always be his and Seth's little sister, that he knew their parents' love and their spirit was here with them today, and that the power and strength of that love had brought them all back together.

I want that kind of love, Marcy thought. The kind that endured fire and time and every hardship life had to offer. She looked at Evan, and realized *she* did have it. The problem was, the person she loved, didn't love her back.

"The boys are looking thirsty." Rand leaned over and gave her a friendly kiss on the cheek, then stood. "Sure I can't get you anything?"

Evan, was her first thought, but she simply smiled and shook her head.

She glanced around the room at the people celebrating, imagined what this room would look like if this was *her* wedding. She could see it clearly in her mind: pink roses, hundreds of them; a four-tiered cake with raspberry filling; a live band that played everything from

Glen Miller to contemporary rock. Her dress would be organza, with satin ribbons and a full skirt.

And a tiara, she thought, smiling. What woman could resist a tiara?

A commotion from the corner of the room jolted Marcy out of her daydream. One of the guests, an attractive blonde, had spilled a glass of champagne on the photographer and she was profusely apologizing. Marcy knew that it was rare for any wedding not to have a problem of some kind, but a spilled glass of champagne would hardly be considered a crisis.

Still, years of catering and party planning were in her blood. She started to wave for a member of the staff to help, but suddenly three little girls had hold of her arms and were pulling her out to the dance floor. Grinning, Evan grabbed her shoulders and kissed her square on the mouth.

"Evan Carver!" Marcy gasped, then looked down at the little girls, who were all giggling.

"They dared me to kiss you." Evan winked at the girls. "I can't very well turn down a dare. I'd look like a sissy."

Rolling her eyes, Marcy glanced at the children and with her finger, made a circle by her head. Laughing, the girls ran off.

"I'm crazy, all right." He pulled her into his arms when a slow song started. "Crazy 'bout you."

Her heart jumped, even though she knew he didn't mean it the way she wanted him to mean it. But it sounded wonderful, so she held on to him, bare feet and all, and slowly swayed to the Eagles' "I Can't Tell You Why."

"Let's get out of here," he said, brushing his lips over her ear.

She lifted her head and looked at him, saw the dark desire shining in his eyes. "The party's not over."

"Close enough. We'll see Jacob and Clair tomorrow morning before—" He stopped, then slid his hand down her back. "Come upstairs with me."

She knew he'd almost said "before you leave." It was easier not to talk about tomorrow, she thought. Easier to just be in the moment.

"All right." She glanced at Jacob and Clair, who were saying goodbye to an elderly couple. "I'll meet you in the hallway."

It took her a few moments to gather her purse and the heels she'd left under the table. She was heading for the hallway when she stopped suddenly, then turned and was drawn back to the double doors leading to the chapel.

She needed to see it one more time, at night. Just for a moment, she told herself and stepped inside. She breathed in the lingering scent of roses, touched each pew as she slowly walked down the aisle, felt the cool tile under her feet.

This chapel was her "baby," she thought, smiling softly. Hers and Evan's. She wanted to embrace what they'd done, etch it in her mind and keep it in her heart.

From the back of the chapel, Evan watched her move up the steps to the spot where Clair and Jacob had said their vows earlier. Moonlight streamed through the stained-glass window and caressed her face, flowed like water over her blue dress.

Like the first time he'd seen her stand there, he simply couldn't think.

Couldn't breathe.

Quietly, he turned and walked away. When he was outside, he dragged a long pull of air into his lungs, then went to the hallway and waited for her.

She woke slowly the next morning, drifted in and out of that warm, comfortable place between sleep and consciousness. It was a lovely place to be, and she thought she could stay there forever, floating, half dreaming. She stirred, felt the solid length of Evan's body against hers. Opening her eyes, Marcy realized he was already awake, his elbow bent, resting his head on his hand while he gazed down at her.

"Mornin'," he said softly.

"Morning." It embarrassed her that he'd been watching her, but in an odd way, it pleased her, as well. Smiling, she pulled the sheet up and snuggled under the covers. "What time is it?"

"Six-thirty."

Groaning, she closed her eyes and burrowed deeper into the mattress. They'd had very little sleep last night. But then reality hit her and she realized what day it was: the last day they would wake up together.

Suddenly six-thirty seemed very, very late.

When his hand skimmed the bare curve of her hip, she shivered. He kissed her, soft and slow, with a tenderness that melted her bones. She wrapped her arms around his neck and kissed him back, until they were both breathing hard and more than a little aroused. His lips still on hers, he rolled her to her back.

"By the way," he said, "I ordered room service."

"Already? It's so—" on a moan, she gripped the bedclothes in her fists when his hands slid to her breasts "—early."

"Yeah, but I'm starving."

He nibbled on her neck, then moved lower. Fire skipped through her blood when his tongue found her hardened nipple.

"How much time do we have?" she asked breathlessly.

"Thirty minutes."

"Wonderful," she murmured, then arched upward, awash in the delicious sensations rippling through her. Restless, she stroked her hands over his back and shoulders, murmuring his name. He kissed her breasts, her hip, her stomach, then moved over her and slid inside. She wrapped herself around him, needing him closer still, felt the desperation rage inside him, dark and wild and raw. It shuddered from his body into hers, then ripped through them both, as sharp as it was fierce.

He filled her. Her body. Her heart. Her soul.

I love you, she nearly said, but managed to hold those three precious words back. She couldn't bear it if he turned away from her now.

It was a long moment before either one of them moved, then he gathered her close and kissed her cheek, then her nose.

"I'll go warm up the shower," he said, his voice still ragged. "Join me?"

"Sure." But she wasn't certain her legs could hold her up at the moment. "In a minute."

She watched him walk to the bathroom, felt her heart tighten and twist. *Later,* she told herself. Don't think about it now.

She sat slowly, dragged a hand through her hair, was reaching for her robe when she heard a knock from the other room. *Room service.* She'd completely forgotten about them, and apparently so had Evan. Pulling her robe on, she padded through the living room and opened the door.

When the camera flashed in her face, she froze.

Ten

Dear Marcy,
I'm giving a fiftieth anniversary party for my parents and though I want to make my own invitations, I'm not very creative and don't know where to start. Can you help me?
Kathy in Aurora

Evan had just opened the shower door when he heard Marcy cry out. He grabbed a towel and flew out of the bathroom, kept moving when she wasn't in the bedroom.

"Get out of here!" Evan heard Marcy yell from the living room. "Leave me alone!"

When he raced around the corner, a flash blinded him for a moment, then he saw the short, balding man standing in the suite entry, his foot shoved against the door while he quickly snapped pictures.

Evan saw red. On a roar, he charged the man, who

managed to snap another picture before he spun on his heels and dashed down the hall.

"Evan, no!"

He felt Marcy grab his arm, but it didn't even slow him down. He tore after the guy, wasn't even halfway down the hall before the man was already inside the elevator.

Dammit, dammit, dammit! Evan yelled at the man, who actually had the nerve to grin and wave as the doors were starting to close. Son of a bitch! He'd never catch him now!

Later, Evan would realize that the woman who seemed to appear out of nowhere had actually stepped out of the suite closest to the elevators. But at that moment, the only thing he really noticed was a blonde in gray sweatpants and a white tank top move in front of the elevator and slam her hand on the doors to keep them from closing. The grin on the man's face turned to shock as the blonde stepped onto the elevator and snatched the camera.

"Hey!" the guy hollered and grabbed at the woman. In one fluid move, she had the guy's hand in hers and he was on his knees, moaning in pain.

Smiling, the woman tossed the camera to Evan when he reached the elevator. She flicked her gaze downward and arched an eyebrow. "Nice towel."

Adrenaline still pumping, his chest heaving, Evan caught the camera with one hand and held the towel with his other. "Thanks."

"Evan!" Marcy ran up behind him, clutching her robe tightly together. "Are you all right?"

"Better than this jerk." Evan nodded at the photographer, then looked back at Marcy. Her cheeks were pale, her eyes wide and frightened. "You okay?"

"I'm fine. He just surprised me." Marcy stared first at the man on his knees, then at the blonde. "Who are you?"

"You got no right," the man choked out the words while he tried to stand. "I'm going to sue your—"

The woman tweaked the man's hand a fraction, and he went down again, groaning even louder. "I'll be back up in ten minutes." The blonde gave a toss of her long ponytail and reached for the elevator button. "And if it's not too much trouble, do you think you guys could get me some coffee?"

"My name is Shelby Richards." Sitting at the dining-room table in Evan's suite, the woman opened two sugar packets and dumped them in her coffee. No one could have looked at the slender, pretty blonde and imagined that fifteen minutes ago she'd taken down a man with a mere flick of one slim wrist. "I'm a private investigator from Los Angeles."

Marcy sucked in a breath and glanced at Evan. Arms folded, he stood beside the table, clenching his jaw. They'd managed to drag some clothes on before room service had shown up, but Marcy was still too shook up to eat and Evan was still too angry.

"So it's true then?" The knot in Marcy's stomach tightened. "Helen hired you to find me?"

Shelby lifted her coffee and blew on it. "Not exactly."

"Why don't you tell us *exactly* what *is* true?" Evan said tightly.

"She hired me to keep an eye out for your friend, Arnie Blanchard." Shelby eyed a piece of bacon. "Do you mind? I'm starving."

"Arnie Blanchard?" Marcy's eyes widened, then narrowed with anger as she slid the plate of food closer to Shelby. "I thought he looked familiar."

"Do you ladies care to fill me in?" Evan said, frowning. "Or am I supposed to guess?"

"Arnie calls himself a journalist, but he's nothing more than a sleazeball tabloid paparazzi." Shelby munched on the bacon. "He'd been after Marcy here for some time, looking for something to tarnish her shiny, wholesome image."

"Arnie's been after *me?*" Just the thought of it made Marcy's skin crawl. "How do you know this?"

"Helen has her sources," Shelby said.

Evan lifted an eyebrow. "You mean she has you."

"Let's just say I know who to ask what." Shelby rolled a shoulder and finished off the bacon. "But that's irrelevant for this conversation. What is relevant is that Helen knew Arnie had been trying to dig up dirt on Marcy for the past couple of months, especially because of all the PR her new TV show is getting. It would be a real coup to get a scoop on Miss Marcy Pruitt. He nearly got it this morning. Tomorrow's headline in all the media would have probably been Marcy Pruitt's Secret Love Nest, complete with pictures."

Oh, dear Lord. Marcy closed her eyes and drew in a breath to steady herself. Shelby was right. A story and picture like that *would* make news. And if it had, there was no telling what the producer of her show might do.

"So Arnie's been watching me all the time I've been here in Wolf River?" The thought of it sent a chill slithering up Marcy's spine. "Taking pictures of me?"

Shelby shook her head. "He just got here yesterday, and it took him a while to track you down here. I think your new look threw him off. By the way—" Shelby smiled "—you look fantastic. That haircut is so right for you and I love what you—"

When Evan cleared his throat, Shelby glanced up. "Oh, right. Well, anyway, I followed Arnie to the reception last night and kept an eye on him to make sure he wouldn't bother you."

"That was *you* last night." Marcy remembered the commotion in the corner just before she'd gone out on the dance floor with Evan. "You spilled champagne on the photographer."

Shelby nodded. "I distracted him long enough to stop him from following you up here when you both left the reception, but I knew it wouldn't take him long to figure out what room you were in. I've been waiting for him, but he moved a little quicker this morning than I thought he would."

"Too bad I didn't answer the door." Evan's eyes narrowed to slits. "I would have made that camera part of his lower intestines."

"Now *that* would make a picture," Shelby said with a grin. "The manager here had him hauled off to the sheriff's station. They'll keep him locked up for a while, at least until Marcy's left town."

Until she'd left town. Once again, the reality that she was leaving in a few hours hit her like a two-by-four. She glanced at Evan, saw the grim expression on his face. But she couldn't read his eyes. Couldn't tell if Shelby's statement had any impact on him at all.

A thought suddenly occurred to Marcy that made her back stiffen and her insides turn inside out. She glanced quickly around the room, then looked at Shelby. "Did you…are there any, ah—"

"No bugs, if that's what you're thinking." Shelby tilted her head and batted her thick lashes. "What kind of a girl do you think I am?"

An impressive one, Marcy thought, wondering if the woman might teach her that little move that had put Arnie on the floor.

"Look," Shelby said, the teasing tone gone. "I admit I've been aware of where you've been and with whom, but please believe me, I only came here to watch for Arnie and keep him away from you if he showed up. I didn't come here to snoop on you. Helen very specifically told me *not* to tell her what you were doing. She said if you wanted her to know, you'd tell her yourself."

Marcy sighed heavily, then shook her head. "Helen should have told me about Arnie."

"You'll have to take that up with Helen." Shelby eyed the omelette sitting in front of her. "Are you going to eat that?"

"Why don't you take it on your way out?" Evan suggested. "It seems to me your job here is finished."

"That it is." Shelby picked up the plate, then glanced at Marcy. "By the way, I managed to dig up a little dirt on Arnie myself, so unless he wants his own face on the tabloids, he shouldn't be bothering you anymore."

Marcy didn't even want to know, but it did give her a sense of relief that the man wouldn't be hiding around corners or sneaking around her house or office.

"Thank you," Marcy said when Shelby stood. "In spite of the awkwardness of all this, I do appreciate what you've done."

"Just doing my job." Shelby headed for the door. "You ever need anything, Helen's got my number." She looked over her shoulder at Evan. Her gaze lowered and she grinned. "Nice to meet you, Evan."

Marcy supposed at any other time, with any other woman, she might have felt a little jealous, but considering the circumstances, and the unexpected blush on Evan's cheeks, all she could do was smile. "Looks like you've got a fan," Marcy said after Shelby closed the door behind her.

Frowning, Evan stared at the door. "All the time, she was right under our noses. Damn, I feel like an idiot."

He shook his head, then reached for Marcy and pulled her into his arms. "You okay?"

"I am now." *Now that you're holding me.*

"When I saw that guy with his foot holding the door while he took your picture, I swear I wanted to kill him."

"Most people who come into contact with Arnie say that." Marcy laid her hands on Evan's chest. "I never dreamed my life would have been interesting enough for him to come after me."

"I've played cards with the sheriff a few times," Evan said. "He might look the other way while I pay my respects to the ass—"

She pressed her fingertips to his lips. "Thank you for the gesture," she said, laying her head on his shoulder. "But it doesn't matter. He won't bother us anymore."

Evan stilled the moment she said the words. She hadn't meant to say "us." She knew there was no "us." Not after today. After all they'd been through, she didn't want their goodbye to be awkward or uncomfortable.

"Why don't you go take a shower while I pack?" Lifting her head, she kept the smile on her lips. "I need to give Helen a call."

Something flickered in Evan's dark gaze, and for a moment, she thought he was going to kiss her. Instead, he dropped his arms and nodded. "All right."

She swallowed the thickness in her throat as he walked toward the bedroom. He stopped at the doorway, then turned and met her gaze. "It's not an easy life you live, Miss Pruitt."

I'd give it up for you, she thought, and she knew she would if he wanted her to. But he hadn't asked, and she couldn't offer. All she could do was nod and smile and pray he couldn't see that her heart was shattering into thousands of tiny little pieces.

The growl of bulldozers and the rumble of cement mixers filled the hot Texas afternoon. Clouds of dust kicked up by the heavy machinery lay like a wool blanket over the construction site and the constant *beep-beep-beep* of a tractor grated not only the dirt, but Evan's nerves, as well.

Almost two weeks on the job and already there'd been nothing but problems. A delay with the surveyor's report, two thunderstorms, a misplaced load of foundation forms. All he needed now were the locusts to come through.

Instead, Tom knocked on the trailer door, then stuck his head in. "The generator's down. I sent James into town to pick up a gasket."

Evan swore hotly and slammed down the cup of coffee he'd been drinking, which spilled onto the blueprints he'd been studying—which made him swear all the more.

The locusts have arrived, he thought, then grabbed a napkin to soak up the coffee.

"So—" Ignoring Evan's outburst, Tom stepped inside the trailer "—how's the foot?"

"Fine." Actually, his foot hurt like a son of a bitch,

but he'd be damned if he'd admit it. He'd broken two toes yesterday when he'd kicked a boulder after arguing twenty minutes with an idiot inspector. Bone against stone—stone wins. "Something I can do for you?"

Tom dropped down on an office chair. "Well, my nail gun's broke."

Evan frowned. "And you're telling me this because…?"

Tom tipped his hard hat back from his sweaty face. "I figured I could stuff a box of nails in your mouth and you could spit 'em out for me."

Evan turned to glare at his foreman. "Are you trying to make me mad?"

"Don't have to." Tom stretched out his long legs and crossed one dirt-covered boot over the other. "You're doing that all by yourself."

"I don't know what the hell you're talking about." *Nor do I want to know,* Evan thought and turned back to the blueprints. "We're already behind schedule here, Tom. You of all people should know what that costs us."

"And you of all people should know what happens when a crew walks off a site."

Evan looked up sharply. "Who's walking off?"

"No one," Tom said. "Not yet, anyway. But you keep snarling like a junkyard dog and they will."

Evan's first instinct was to tell Tom to go to hell, but he bit back the words. In his gut, he knew damn well that his foreman was right. He *had* been taking his bad mood out on everyone around him.

And in his gut, he knew damn well why.

Marcy.

He couldn't get the woman out of his mind. Not a day, an hour, barely a *minute* went by he didn't think about her. In two weeks, he hadn't slept one night, hadn't cared about food and didn't give a damn about his work.

He missed her. Missed waking up next to her every morning. Missed her smile, her laugh, the way her lips pursed when she was deep in thought. He missed discussing his day with her, missed hearing about hers.

Nothing like this had ever happened to him before. No woman had ever turned him inside out and upside down. No woman had ever affected his work. No woman had ever made him think that his trailer was too small.

Too lonely.

He hadn't talked to her since the day she'd left for the airport. He hadn't even driven her there—she'd insisted that Shelby was driving there anyway and it was silly for her not to ride with the woman.

He should have argued, dammit. Should have insisted she let him drive her. But she'd almost seemed as if she was in a hurry to get rid of him. In a hurry to leave, to go back to her life in a fishbowl. Her life where fans rushed her in train stations, where her own manager hired a P.I. to keep track of her, where slimy tabloid reporters followed her halfway across the country just to get a damn story that would hurt her.

He wanted no part of that life.

But he wanted Marcy.

He had no indication how she felt about him. She knew his number, and she hadn't called. And he hadn't been able to bring himself to call her, knew that she was getting ready for her TV show. She'd be in meetings, or rehearsals or book signings. The last thing she needed was him bothering her for no other reason than to say hello. To hear her voice.

With a sigh, he dropped down in a chair beside Tom. "Junkyard dog, huh?"

Tom nodded. "With fleas."

Hell. Evan scrubbed a hand over his face, realized he hadn't shaved in a while, though he wasn't certain how long.

He had to do something, that much he knew.

The tough part was figuring out what.

"Ten minutes to air everyone." Sean Monahan, director of *The Real Life With Marcy Pruitt* show, waved a clipboard, then looked at Marcy. "How you doing?"

Marcy smiled and nodded calmly at the director, even though her stomach was fluttering and her hands shaking. Behind her, Helen and Anna were fussing over last-minute changes on the prop table, while the cameramen and soundmen made adjustments with their equipment.

Deep breaths, she reminded herself, then closed her eyes while the makeup artist dusted her face with fresh powder. Today would not only be her maiden show, *live* from Los Angeles, it would also be the national unveiling of the "new" Marcy Pruitt. Today could very well be the day that would make—or break—her career.

And if all that wasn't difficult enough, the producer had brought in a test audience for Marcy to interact with during the show. If she wasn't afraid she'd ruin her crisp, mint-green blouse and khaki skirt, she just might throw up.

Instead, she concentrated on her breathing, slowly felt herself relax as she imagined herself on a deserted beach. Aqua blue water. Warm sand. The gentle lap of waves on the shore. She was wonderfully, blissfully alone.

But then suddenly she wasn't alone. Evan was with her. Lying on a towel beside her, his skin bronzed and damp from swimming, his dark hair slicked back. She smiled at him, reached out to touch him.

And he vanished.

Fool, she thought, not certain if she meant herself or Evan. Maybe both.

"Don't frown, sweetie," Trixie, the makeup artist warned. "You'll get wrinkles."

What do I care? Marcy thought. What were a few wrinkles compared to a broken heart? When she'd left Wolf River, she hadn't thought she could possibly hurt more than she had that day.

She'd been so wrong.

She hadn't heard from Evan, though idiot that she was, she jumped every time her cell phone rang, eagerly checked her messages at home every night, hoping, wishing…

Apparently, he had moved on easily enough.

"Five minutes!"

Her eyes flew open and her stomach twisted into little knots. But strangely enough, she preferred this piercing arrow of fear to the overwhelming pain she felt when she was alone. The only thing that had saved her since she'd returned home had been her work. Her work gave her a reason to get up in the morning, to force herself to smile and act like nothing was wrong, when inside her heart was aching.

"Marcy." Helen hurried toward her, then slipped an arm around her waist. "Honey, I need to talk with you."

"Now? But we've only got—"

"It's important." Helen pulled her away from Trixie. "I just want you to know how proud I am of you."

"Thank you." Marcy glanced nervously at the director, who didn't seem concerned they had only four minutes till airtime.

"I know I don't always make the best choices for you." Helen took Marcy's hands in hers. "But I promise you I only have the best of intentions."

"Helen, we've already settled all this between us," Marcy said quietly. "I understand why you hired Shelby, and it's fine. We've agreed, you won't do anything like that again, and you won't keep things from me. Right?"

"Right." Helen smiled, then squeezed Marcy's hands. "I only want you to be happy, sweetheart."

The sudden moisture in Helen's eyes stunned Marcy. In four years, she'd never seen Helen cry. Not once.

"Stop that," Marcy said firmly. "This is no time to get emotional on me. I'm going on live television, for heaven's sake."

"That's my girl." Helen blinked back her tears, then quickly composed herself and squeezed Marcy's hands. "Now go knock their socks off."

As the director counted down, Marcy stood on her mark behind the kitchen work counter where most of the show took place. She'd be reading from a tele-prompter for the opening, so the most important thing for her to remember was which camera to look at when.

"Ready…" The director held up his hand. "Five, four, three…"

Marcy slowly drew in a breath, slowly released it, and smiled. "…two, one—" the director pointed at her "—and you're *on*!"

"Welcome to *The Real Life With Marcy Pruitt*," Marcy said after the applause died down. "I'm Marcy Pruitt, your host for the next hour. Now some of you may be shaking your heads and saying, that's not Marcy Pruitt. I know what Marcy Pruitt looks like and that's not her." Marcy picked up her glasses sitting on the counter in front of her and put them on. "Recognize me now?"

She explained that she'd decided it was time for the

"Ultimate Marcy Makeover" on herself, and she hoped everyone liked her new look, then asked everyone to let her know, either by phone or mail or on her Web site.

"On our first show today," she said, "we'll be designing homemade invitations for that special occasion, baking brownie cookies and learning how to extend the vase life of cut flowers. So stay right where you are and we'll be right back."

When they cut to a commercial, Marcy dragged in a big gulp of air, waved at the clapping audience, then moved to her mark for her first segment, which was the handmade invitations.

So far so good.

The director cued her, and once again, she was smiling into a live camera. "Our first project today is handmade invitations," she said, "and I'm going to take you step-by-step through our first sample, a wedding invitation."

Marcy reached for the invitation, realized that while it was handmade, it wasn't the one she'd created for the show. *My first crisis on live TV,* she thought, struggling to remain calm. Smiling, she held the invitation and described the layered effect of lace, torn paper and pearl beads on the outside while the camera zoomed in for a closeup. When she opened the card, her heart stopped.

A tiny paper bird popped up, and underneath the bird, in large letters:

Evan Carver and Marcy Pruitt would like you to
join them in their wedding ceremony, any month,
any day, any time of Marcy's choice.
As long as it's soon.
Evan Carver

Was this a joke? she thought, too dazed to move. No
one would be that cruel. She heard applause, heard the
murmurs of excited voices, but she was still too numb
to respond. She simply stood there, staring at the invitation, until she felt someone—Helen—touch her
shoulder and tell her to look up.

When she did, she saw him.

Heart pounding, Marcy watched a man wearing a suit
and tie stand up from his seat in the back row of the audience. *Evan!* The cameras followed him as he walked
down the steps toward her, carrying a bouquet of red roses.

She couldn't speak, couldn't breathe. He stopped in
front of her and handed her the roses, then took her hand
and pulled her from behind the counter.

When he dropped down on one knee, she thought for
certain she would faint.

"Marcy Pruitt." He looked straight into her eyes,
pulled a small black velvet box out of his pants pocket,
opened it, then held it up. "Will you marry me?"

Will you marry me?

She stared at him, then looked at the audience. Every

woman in the room, including herself, seemed to be holding their breath. Marcy quickly glanced at Helen and Anna, who were hugging each other and smiling.

She'd have to talk to them about this later.

At the moment, though, she was a little busy.

Marcy stared at the diamond solitaire Evan offered her, could feel her heart vibrating through her entire body.

"Marry you?" was the best she could manage.

"Marry me," he repeated softly, then took the ring and slid it on her finger. "Please."

"I—" she swallowed the tears in her throat "—I— yes!" she gasped, then threw her arms around him. "Yes!"

He kissed her then, as if no one else in the world was there. No audience, no cameramen, no two hundred thousand television viewers sitting in their living rooms. And she kissed him back.

The audience was on their feet, clapping and cheering. Over the thunderous applause, Sean, the director, stepped to the camera and said, "*The Real Life With Marcy Pruitt* will be right back after this commercial, folks. Stay with us."

Sean turned to Evan. "We'll have three minutes of commercial here, then five minutes of on-air setup with the producer before we bring Marcy back to the stage. That's eight minutes. Not one second more."

Marcy wrapped her arms around Evan's neck when he lifted her off her feet and carried her behind the set. Before she could speak, his mouth was on hers again, kissing her, driving out every other thought. She couldn't think, but she could feel.

Lord, how she could feel. Her heart swelled in her chest, blossomed like the roses she still held in her hand.

"I love you," he said against her lips.

"I love you, too." She was still reeling, still confused. And incredibly happy. "But how did you…when did you—"

He put a finger to her lips. "I was going crazy without you. And making everyone around me crazy, too. I think if I hadn't come here myself, my crew would have tied me up and mailed me."

"I could have lived with that," Marcy said with a smile.

He grinned at her. "The point is, I can't live without you. I don't want to. And if that means being part of all this—" he nodded toward the set "—then fine."

"Evan, you just proposed to me on television." She touched his cheek, knew that the seconds were flying by before she'd have to be in front of the camera again. "Why—and how?"

"Why, because I decided to face head-on the one thing that I didn't think I could handle, which was being in the spotlight. I figured if I could do this and survive, and if you'd have me, then the rest would be a piece of cake. And the how—" he shrugged "—well, I called Helen and she took care of that."

"Helen?" Marcy looked over her shoulder, was surprised the woman wasn't peeking around the corner. "This was Helen's idea?"

"She ran it by the producer and we all collaborated," Evan said.

So that's why Helen had been acting so odd just before the show, Marcy realized. She wasn't sure whether she should fire her manager or give her a raise.

"You mean conspired," Marcy said, arching an eyebrow.

"Whatever it took to make you say yes." He brushed his lips lightly over hers. "I wasn't sure if you'd have room for me in your life. I didn't want to give you time to think about it."

"You really don't know?" she said softly, touching his cheek. "I'd have walked away from everything for you. I still would, if you asked me to."

"And deprive your fans of brownie recipes and tips on cutting flowers?" He smiled at her. "I'll share you during the day, Miss Pruitt. But at night—" he pulled her closer "—at night, baby, you're all mine."

Just the thought of it made her heart sing. "But what about your business? How will you—"

"Jacob's giving up the P.I. business. He wants to settle down now that he's married. He and Tom will run Carver Construction in Texas, and I'll run a branch here."

"You're going to live here—in L.A.?" She could

barely hear him through the symphony playing in her head. "And work here?"

"Well, of course I am." He frowned at her. "Why wouldn't I live where my wife lives?"

Wife. The reality of it all sank in and she had to blink the tears back. Any minute now, she would have to be on camera again. She didn't dare cry now.

Later, she told herself. Later, she'd need an entire tissue box.

"And anyway," Evan said, "your little canyon cottage is big enough for two, isn't it?"

"Actually," she said a bit sheepishly, "it's not that little. It's more like five thousand square feet."

"Five thousand?" He whistled softly. "Well, then, I suppose we won't have to add on when we have babies, will we?"

Wife. Babies. That did it. She couldn't stop the tears.

He held her close, pressed his mouth to her temple. "Say when and where, sweetheart."

"We'll talk about when later, when I can think straight. As for the where—" She lifted her head and through the blur of her tears met his gaze. "I know this great little chapel in Texas."

Smiling, he kissed the tip of her nose. "I was hoping you'd say that."

"Marcy!" Helen stuck her head around the corner. "The phone lines are jammed and so is your Web site. Everyone loves you!"

If Helen hadn't left as quickly as she'd popped up, Marcy might have told her that she only needed one person to love her.

And that person, Marcy thought as she kissed Evan again, was in her arms.

* * * * *

Look for BLACKHAWK LEGACY,
Dillon Blackhawk's story,
coming in December from Silhouette Books.

From bestselling author

BEVERLY BARTON

Laying His Claim

(Silhouette Desire #1598)

After Kate and Trent Winston's daughter was kidnapped, their marriage collapsed from the trauma. Ten years later, Kate discovers that their daughter might still be alive. Amidst their intense search, Kate and Trent find something else they'd lost: hot, passionate sexual chemistry. Now, can they claim the happy ending they deserve?

Ready to lay their lives on the line, but unprepared for the power of love!

Available August 2004 at your favorite retail outlet.

If you enjoyed what you just read,
then we've got an offer you can't resist!

Take 2 bestselling love stories FREE!

Plus get a FREE surprise gift!

COMING NEXT MONTH

#1597 STEAMY SAVANNAH NIGHTS—Sheri WhiteFeather
Dynasties: The Danforths
Bodyguard Michael Whittaker was intensely drawn to illegitimate
Danforth daughter Lea Nguyen. He knew she was keeping secrets
and Michael's paid pursuit soon spilled into voluntary overtime. They
couldn't resist the Savannah heat that burned between them, yet could
they withstand the forces that were against them?

#1598 LAYING HIS CLAIM—Beverly Barton
The Protectors
After Kate and Trent Winston's daughter was kidnapped, their marriage
collapsed from the trauma. Ten years later, Kate discovered that their
daughter might still be alive. Amidst their intense search, Kate and Trent
found something else they'd lost: hot, passionate sexual chemistry. Now,
could they claim the happy ending they deserved?

#1599 BETWEEN DUTY AND DESIRE—Leanne Banks
Mantalk
A promise to a fallen comrade had brought marine corporal
Brock Armstrong to Callie Newton's home. He'd vowed to help the
widow move on with her life, but he'd had no idea Callie would call
to him so deeply, placing Brock in the tense position between duty and
desire.

#1600 PERSUADING THE PLAYBOY KING—Kristi Gold
The Royal Wager
Playboy prince Marcel Frederic DeLoria bet his Harvard buddies
that he'd still be unattached by their tenth reunion. But when he was
unexpectedly crowned, the sweet and sexy Kate Milner entered his
kingdom. Could Kate persuade this playboy king to lose his royal wager?

#1601 STONE COLD SURRENDER—Brenda Jackson
Madison Winters was never one for a quick fling, but when she met
sexy Stone Westmoreland, the bestselling author taught the proper
schoolteacher a lesson worth learning: when it came to passion, even
the most sensible soul could lose their sensibilities.

#1602 AWAKEN TO PLEASURE—Nalini Singh
Stunningly sexy Jackson Santorini couldn't wait to call a one-on-one
conference with his former secretary, Taylor Reid. But—despite his
tender touch—Taylor was tentative to enter into a romantic liaison.
Could Jackson seduce the bedroom-shy Taylor and successfully awaken
her to pleasure?

SDCNM0704